Links

Links

What happens when…?

Dianne Stadhams

Bridge House

British Library Cataloguing in Publication Data
A Record of this Publication is available from the British
Library

ISBN 978-1-907335-63-1

This edition published 2019 by Bridge House Publishing
Manchester, England

All Bridge House books are published on paper derived
from sustainable resources.

Contents

Preface

LINKS... random, unplanned, consequential... shape our journey from cradle to grave.

LUCKY LINKS describes the chain of events from a child-eating crocodile in Africa to sexual frissons during a global marketing campaign for fair trade footwear. An African community lives with the impact of tourism development and global connections; high flying European business people battle their own monsters; while love comes in many forms and blindness can be more than physical.

DRAMATIC LINKS is about choice... the costs and the benefits. Set in an English country village, narrated by Nosey Nolan, a prodigal academic and highlighting the politics of village amateur dramatics, the question is who stabbed the leading lady in the Wyeway pantomime and why?

LITERARY LINKS offers a gourmet mixture of biography with recipes for life, love and laughter. Six women, of different ages, from different worlds discover connections and catharsis when Kesia Jaskins publishes her book, *An Appetite for Words*. Meet a best-selling English author, an African campaigner against female genital mutilation, a lost property worker with a speech impediment, a waitress confronting domestic violence, a charity shop manager and an orphan with a love of literature.

LINKS has been inspired by my consultancy work in sub-Saharan Africa on sustainable development issues: my experience as an urban émigré to a small English village: and my passion as a writer.

I adore black humour and the opportunity to challenge conventional genres and perspectives.

ENJOY

Acknowledgments

Dianne is particularly grateful to Gill James and all at Bridge House Publishing for their support, guidance and encouragement in producing this collection.

Thanks are also due to John Tolson for the photograph "Literary Links".

LUCKY LINKS

Crocodiles and Chickens

To be or not to be?

Man it was sure not a snap decision to be a celebrity. It just sort of fell at my feet – fame was flung and postcards printed. Camera clicks... my enigmatic smile... my perfect jaw line... my glistening orthodontics... a skin to die for... a torso toned and triggered. Guess that makes this dude an icon... in water and on land.

The game begins. Decisions... decisions will have to be taken. Mine or yours? Backwards or forwards? Linear or profile? Who first? What's best? When's right?

I've heard it all in the last few months and then some. Facts and fantasies of the guide as she shepherds the tourists beside my vantage spot, their eyes agog.

"Do you know his descendants can be traced back 200 million years?"

Dudes the family resemblance is uncanny.

"Did you know his family have been worshipped?"

Fear and respect inspire legends.

"Can you guess his weight? His speed? His vital statistics?"

The banal assumes elevated status.

The golfers are more pragmatic.

"Does he return the golf balls?"

Beware, oh my voyeurs. Myths are rooted in fact. Wisdom has it that my family are guardians of knowledge. Remember to respect that wisdom lest it swallow you whole. Artists have immortalised my family as symbols of sunrise and fertility. My ancestors grabbed the foolish and ate the guilty without a trial.

Ignorance will not protect you from certainty.

Because that's what we crocodiles do... and have always done... for the last 200 million years... and are likely to keep doing unless you dumb humans kill off the planet.

And just for the record – I'm called Atta Gatta, I'm four metres long, weigh 100 kilograms, and my best time on land is 17 kilometres an hour. Although I am prepared to admit the chance of my running for any longer than five minutes is extremely unlikely. Celebrity dudes like me prefer to pose. Especially as these marketing-savvy, politically-correct, flora-and-fauna-conscious kebabs on two legs at the golf course have constructed a palatial lake as my home away from home.

"Water hazard or what!" those golfers say as if it was an original joke.

Want to get into the water and say it direct?

Golfers and crocodiles have more in common than you might think. Focus is our motto, timing our creed. A golfer locates the target and fixes his gaze, all the while assessing distance, ground covered and potential obstacles to the flight of that ball. Crocodiles target their location and gaze upon their fix... obstacles can be opportunities. A water hazard to a golfer is but a portent to an Atta Gatta.

Golfers and crocodiles admire strength – the golfers to swing and hit their object of desire, crocodiles to grab theirs and run. Our tools of the trade may differ (golfers use clubs and crocs have teeth), but we both know that we have to be precise, measured and accurate to score. Both of us play against ourselves... to win.

Concentrate – one wrong move and it's splash – but not a birdie!

I first noticed the little girl when she crawled into a clump of bushes beside the water hazard. Brave of the kid, tooth-pick scrappy, limbs with no flesh, tangled curls, big eyes with bigger questions. She carried a chicken with long golden feathers tucked under her scrawny shoulder, its staccato head pecking a 180 degree trail as the kid walked.

Hey feather–brain, the gods look after each other. You are not on my icon list.

But the kid didn't offer me the bird. She stroked its crested crown and gently massaged its trembling wattle. She lifted its wing and nudged its head under before folding the wing over.

Is that a yoga approach to fowl calming?

A sort of bird-brain chicken that lost its head but saved its beak. I liked that. Showed respect... even if I wasn't going to get a chicken wing bite... so to speak.

The girl rocked the chicken like a pendulum. It went silent. So did she. But her eyes stayed fixed on mine. I blinked. Let her know I was watching... and waiting. She blinked back. The chicken kept swinging.

Check, honey, your move.

Crocodile chess is not a game for an amateur. Humans boast that they have their memories. Human brains may be larger and more complex. But we crocs have patience evolved over megatime... DNA coded... watch and wait. We know if we wait long enough you humans become careless. Dangle a limb over the side of a boat to cool in the water. Take your eye of the ball. Forget to check behind you.

Patience is the patron saint of reptiles.

The girl moves closer. The chicken remains silent. I blink – fast.

Her move.

She winks – slowly.

My move.

I leave the starter block. The jaws are tight. I roll twice in the water. The kid tries to scream. The scream becomes a gurgle. Marinated chick-kid equals check-mate!

Uncertain certainty... a sure thing... dead right.

Crocodile tears you call them. Me, I put them down to indigestion. Feathers and femurs are an eclectic starter. What's that adage?

A bird in the bush is worth two… chomp, chomp…

"Hey Graham, knock, knock."

"Who's there?" replies Graham, the golfer.

"Chicken," says his partner.

"Chicken who?" says Graham.

The golfer has lost his ball. He's convinced it's not in the water. He heads towards the bushes.

New game started.

"Chick-en the bushes," says the golfer. They laugh.

Pawn to king dude. Take-away to rook.

A celebrity croc won't look a gift horse in the mouth.

Food parcel to check mate. Nothing but death is certain.

So agree crocodiles and golfers.

"You got Marguerite a present yet?" asks Graham.

His partner shakes his head and says, "I need to find something exotic for that arm candy of mine."

"And expensive," says Graham. "She'll expect the unexpected – big time, big bucks."

"Such as?"

"Diamond-studded handbag made from elephant-scrotum – perfect for your girlfriend."

"Gross," comes the reply. "Graham, you've got a seriously sick sense of humour!"

Candy is dandy when it don't make you sick.

Children scream from behind the bushes… the golfers rush forward… a grand finale!

A hole in one you might say!

Flip-Flop and Fly

"We make the goodest of good flip-flops[1] sir. Best in village, the bestest of all villages in this area," Urday's boss said to the European visitors. "Time to see best factory."

"What is this boy's name?" asked one of the visitors.

"Hello Urday," whispered the floor manager boss to the deputy boss who spoke to the factory boss.

"Urday," said the boss to the foreigners.

"Urday," said the foreigners to the boy.

The factory boss spoke to the deputy boss who turned to the floor manager boss and whispered an order to the boy.

"Urday," shouted Urday, smiling at them again.

Why do foreigners want to know my name? Is the boss man angry that I talk direct to the white men?

One of the foreigners held out his hand to shake with Urday.

"Call me Graham," he said.

As if!

The foreigners smiled. One checked his watch. The boss pointed to Urday. The boy stepped forward and recited parrot-perfect English, hands-crossed with a large smile.

"We make good flip-flops from dead tyres."

"Dead?" said call-me-Graham.

"No can use no more," explained Urday's boss. "Tyre no good to car, truck, tractor. Too dangerous keep on car. Take tyre off car. Put dead tyre in dump at end of village. Cart dead tyre to here factory. Him wash tyre. Them cut tyre into bits. Me work on bits – punch holes for straps."

---

[1] Flip-flops are a very basic type of footwear — essentially a thin rubber sole with two simple straps running in a Y from the sides of the foot to the join between the big toe and next toe.

"Ah, sustainable development," said call-me-Graham, "recycling."

"No, wrong," said the boss. "We no use bicycles. Tyre from bicycle too skinny – no good. Break easy."

"I think we're talking at cross purposes," call-me-Graham said to his colleagues. "Same thing – dead tyres to cheap sandals equals recycling. Fairtrade footwear we can all agree?"

"Good sound bite," said another of the foreigners, and smiled.

All the visitors nodded and smiled. The factory boss grinned. The deputy boss and the floor manager boss half-smiled.

Urday smiled broadly.

Happy foreigners… happy bosses… all is good… still got my job… lucky day!

"How old is Urday?" asked call-me-Graham.

"Sixteen," whispered the floor manager boss to the deputy boss who spoke to the factory boss.

"Sixteen," said the boss to the white men.

"Sixteen?" said call-me-Graham.

"Sixteen!" said another. "Do pigs fly?"

Is the white man mad? Has he been too long on the golf course in the sun? Pigs fly?

"He's small for his age," added the boss to the white men.

"We have a very strong policy on child labour," said one of the foreigners. "Please ask the boy to tell us directly how old he is."

The boss spoke to his deputy, but not in English. The deputy boss spoke to his factory manager, but not in English or the language used by the boss to his deputy. Finally the factory manager called out to the boy in yet another tongue.

16

Urday breathed deeply and spoke clearly in his best English. "Sixteen," he said proudly, "all healthy."

Everyone smiled at each other.

Why do white men wanted to know how many sisters I got?

Urday smiled at everyone.

What about my brothers?

There were six of them if you only counted the live ones. Ten if you included the ones in the cemetery.

"Please ask Urday how many hours he works each day," said call-me-Graham.

The floor manager boss frowned. He turned to his deputy and translated. His deputy turned to the factory boss and spoke in another dialect.

"Eight," said Urday.

Why are they asking how many hours I spend away from the factory each day?

Urday did not smile any more.

Do they think I am lazy working sixteen hours?

Urday frowned.

What will happen to my family if I lose my job?

Urday swallowed nervously.

These questions are not on the script that the boss made me learn.

The foreign buyers began their strange questions again.

Why do they want to know how many days that I don't come to the factory? What do I say are my favourite days? All days are the same – work, work, work. What is this game?

The foreigners beckoned to Urday as they spoke amongst themselves. The factory boss did not look pleased. He shouted to Urday, "Remember the rules, boy."

As if I'd forget. This job is my life.

"It seems to be a fair trade set up," said call-me-Graham.

"The boy says himself he's sixteen years old, healthy, works eight hours a day and has two days off," said another.

"And we're here – seen the factory. It's light. There's clean air. Food is provided," said a third.

Urday stood silent and politely stared at the ground.

The foreigners got it all wrong.

"This is a good place to take the pictures, with him – Urday – you think?" said one of the men.

"Potential face for the publicity campaign back home?" another asked.

The factory manager took Urday to the side while the foreigners met with the factory boss and his deputy.

"Will you tell the big boss man that them foreigners got the information wrong?" asked Urday.

"You like your job, boy?" replied the manager.

Urday went silent. The bosses and the foreigners talked and talked. Urday stayed silent. Finally the big boss man clapped his hands together. Everyone cheered.

The foreigners shook hands with all the bosses.

"Time is money," said call-me-Graham.

"Time we need to head off to the golf course," said another.

"Ah fair trade and good golf – perfect day," said the boss.

All the foreigners laughed. The factory boss escorted them to his Mercedes. The workers all waved farewell.

Just like the rehearsal! Urday was confused.

"What went wrong?" he asked the floor manager. The man shook his head but said nothing. He pointed towards the door.

Unlucky day – there goes my job. Urday walked out of the office, across the yard, out the gate and down the hill, turning right at the bottom. He walked under the corrugated tin lean-to and sat on the ground. His punch lay beside the rubber straps just as he had left them.

"How go?" asked one of the other boys.

"Maybe no good," said Urday. "The men from Europe not buy."

"Same old, same old, happens every year," said another boy. "Big pretend game. Them bosses don't want to show foreigners real factory, real workers."

"You think they will buy big order?" asked Urday.

"Hey, they ask you questions about your family?"

"Yes," said Urday, "but they take out no flip-flops"

"The boss sweet talk after. Then they buy. Big order. Me get paid. You get paid," explained the boy. "Boss and buyers go play golf?"

Urday nodded.

"Good sign."

"What you learn from them people?" asked another boy.

"Strange stuff," said Urday, "Mzungu[2] think pigs fly. Their money is called time."

"Weird, hey Urday? You got to wonder about them faraway places."

"The teacher showed us a book with pigs standing on the ground," said Urday.

"Sure," said the boy," but the Imam says no pigs in our village. So what does that teacher really know?"

"I'm going to ask my friend, Jonah," said Urday.

"You think that Mzungu knows everything," said the boy.

"Not everything," said Urday, "but lots. Jonah sure knows about foreign stuff."

"Last year them foreigners said that money can buy anything where they come from," said a boy.

"So how come them Mzungu visit here to buy dead tyre shoes to wear?" asked Urday.

---

[2] Mzungu is Swahili for a white foreigner.

None of the workers had an answer.

"I want to be a tourist when I grow up," said Urday. "Eat, drink, golf all day. Travel the world, play, have fun, see flying pigs."

"You going to wear flip-flops?" they laughed.

"If I get lucky," agreed Urday, "my flip-flops will fly!"

Hoodies and Hijabs

I hate birthdays.

In my family a birthday is a misnomer for a "dead-darling" day. Whatever happens to other people on their birthdays doesn't work for us. We get a kind of upside down, inside out, back to front celebration. In my family when it's your time to have a birthday you lie down with cloves of garlic nailed to the bed, a fetish around your ankle and fingers crossed not to sleep... until it's all over... one way or the other.

"Garlic on the bed head? What next – elephant dung under the pillow?" my Pa mocked on the eve of his forty-fifth. He ordered my Ma to remove the protection. My Pa didn't wake up.

"He's dead, darling," said my Ma.

And not just my Pa. My uncle died on his birthday – bitten by a snake. My first aunt got out of bed, ate her birthday breakfast with an up-yours-darling smile... and fell sideways off the chair. They said she was dead before she hit the floor. The celebrations were cancelled. Ma said we could use my aunt's birthday cake for the funeral. But it took 60 hours from birthday party to burial pit. The cake got weevils. Nobody would eat it. Ma fed the remains, weevils and all, to the hens. Their chicks were born with extra length feathers and super-wart wattles.

I could keep going as fifteen of my close family have departed this world on those bad days, their dead-darling days. My theory is that our family are mutants... with a genetic trigger cocked for birthdays.

But this story is not about my family history and its genetic dysfunction. It's about the big question – luck. Girl or boy – who is the luckier? When a girl is born the old men in the village say to the father, "Better luck next time!"

My Ma says to the fathers, "You are a lucky one. A daughter will be there to hold your hand when you die."

And so it starts with my sister's sixth birthday. My aunt, Sinitta, who lives in London, sent money for her present. It was a pet chicken with long golden feathers... and a red wattle with so many purple warts it was impossible to agree on the total. It was one supreme-ugly bird but my sister loved it on sight. Personally I would have denied ownership of something so hideous. But I digress – a birthday present is a gift after all.

Party games like *Snap* and *I Spy* take on a whole new meaning when your sister gets eaten by a crocodile. Atta Gatta, the crocodile that lives in the water hazard on the nearby golf course, got lucky with the chicken (a boy) and my sister (a girl... obviously). We don't know if it was a boy or a girl crocodile. It seemed to me that the crocodile scored top points with a double whammy birthday deal.

Eat one, get one free.

Nobody ate anything that day or at her departed-day ceremony. I guess there is no advantage in being a girl or a boy with a crocodile around.

I watched the grab and gobble fiasco from up in the tree behind the bushes next to the water hazard. It was my first day of wearing the hijab. I was twelve years, three months and six days old.

"Nala, today is your first-fortune day," Ma had said when she gave it to me to wear. "You are now a woman."

"Welcome," Ma's friends said.

Welcome? Worry is more like it!

What if there is a connection between first-fortune and dead-darling days?

In DBH (days before hijab) I could climb a tree before my sister could count to ten. I always beat Urday. Urday says it's luck. But that's just Urday trying to act cool. Because

Urday and me both know I am the better tree climber… and runner… and jumper-over-fences. I am better than Urday at everything from school to sport. Which has to be more than luck as Urday is eight months, four days and fifty-eight minutes older than me. He is also three hands-stretched-open, taller. Urday and me have been friends forever. My Ma and his bent together beside the river in the village to wash clothes. Us turbo-charged, grubby kids went too. Fences and trees were our first challenges. The boys were fast but clumsy with bravado. Us girls cautiously tottered in our bid for freedom. It was not luckier to be a boy or a girl on the move as your ma always caught you before it got really interesting. But Urday and me learnt that if you waited for a brother or sister to head off first, there was a degree of half-luck as your ma chased a sibling before she got round to you.

I worked out that girls could create their own luck, whatever those old men said. But DWH (days with hijab) changed the odds. Tree climbing, running and jumping all took longer. And that's after you work out what you can see and where to run and jump – hijabs are handicaps!

When Urday turned up at my house wearing a hoodie my Ma was unhappy.

"A hoodie," she said.

"Latest – like it?" Urday said to Ma.

"No," said my Ma. "What is wrong with what your father wears?"

She might be a woman but she's definitely not subtle.

"Time for change," said Urday.

"Change does not bring luck," argues Ma.

"Maybe…" says Urday.

Yeah, whatever, like they're ever going to agree.

"Today is a day to take care and give thanks for our blessings. Today I have one daughter with six years of life behind her, and thanks be to Allah, six and sixty ahead."

"Happy birthday, little one," smiles Urday.

My sister shows him her present.

"Am I invited for a chicken dinner?" he asks her. She shrieks and places the chicken under her arm. We all laugh. My sister knows Urday is joking.

"Today my other daughter is also blessed. Today Nala starts to wear her hijab," Ma announces proudly.

Urday looks at me and winks when Ma is not looking. That wink is my challenge. He thinks my luck has changed. The handicap has been granted.

"Nala," he says, "hijabs cannot run as fast as hoodies."

My sister starts to run. Urday and I chase her. The game has started.

"That's hoodie hoodoo," I shout.

Ma calls in alarm, "Hijabs behave like women. Women walk."

So what about hoodies Ma? Do they have boundaries?

In DBH I might have been able to scramble down the tree and run faster to beat Urday to the crocodile. But that day I learnt that a hijab is not less lucky than a hoodie. Urday got to the reptile before me. He ripped off his hoodie. He crept forward and threw it over to blind the beast. Confused, the croc paused and then tossed it off. I threw Urday my hijab. He lunged, lassoed the jaws with the hijab and bound them as tightly as he could. The crocodile lashed its tail, trying to smack Urday sideways. But Urday was quick like a flea and hung onto the tail – this way and that.

I screamed.

Urday hollered.

Mzungu – white golfing men – appeared, startled by the commotion.

"Bloody hell," said one of them.

"Mobile, Graham, give me the mobile phone," screamed another.

A third golfer ran towards Urday and the crocodile with his golf club. He smashed it down on the beast's head. Stunned, the crocodile froze for a moment.

"Geez... it's got a bit of flesh in its teeth," shrieked Graham, dropping his mobile phone.

That's my sister you're talking about!

One man threw a golf club at Urday. He caught it. Between them they pulverized the croc's brain. The beast shuddered to a stop. What a scene – blood and brains splattered everywhere – on the ground, the golf clubs, the hoodie and my hijab. They saved Urday but not my sister and her chicken. I told Urday later that the best luck a hoodie or a hijab could have was a golf club. Especially on a dead-darling day!

"You two were damn brave," said one of the golfers.

"Or bloody mad," said another. "Weren't you scared?"

Urday stared... and said nothing. I looked at Urday and then studied the ground.

Foreigners can be just as scary as crocodiles.

"Hey, Graham isn't that the kid from the factory?"

"Don't know," replied Graham. "Hard to tell. These kids all look the same."

"Urday," said the foreigner. "Hey kid, is your name Urday?"

Urday looked at the man. The golfer repeated Urday's name. Urday put him out of his misery and nodded. The men walked towards us. They hugged Urday, saying his name over and over. They turned towards me. Urday jumped in front of me, preventing them from touching. Ma would have been proud. I felt lucky that their hands had not defiled me. What penance I would have had to pay – a first-fortune day with my honour questioned.

"Hey Urday, you and your friend play golf?"

As if... you have to pay to play that game.

25

"You've got a great swing Urday," one said. "You're a natural – calm, strong, accurate."

"We should recommend the kid for the publicity campaign," said Graham. "He'd get paid a shed load more than making those flip-flops."

The men outlined their ideas to Urday in theatrical pidgin-English. I asked Urday why he didn't tell them he had won second prize in English for the school. He told me he would lose his job if he spoke English to foreign visitors.

"Stay silent," he said in our village language. "Be strong."

My Ma says the strength of women is on their lips and in their ears.

"Flip-flops fly?" asked Urday.

"It's your lucky day boy," said the golfer called Graham.

So maybe the boy in the hoodie got lucky?

"Fantastic souvenir," said Graham.

But it was my hijab they used to wrap the crocodile skin.

Carrot Juice and Cappuccino

There are worse stains than carrot juice splattered across a beige, raw silk blouson. Double strength cappuccino cascading down a white linen shirt is one.

When Marguerite and Sidney collided in the organic café on the corner of Main Street, the owner of the neighbouring dry cleaners knew his prayer for the day had been answered.

"Oh God, I'm so sorry," he said.

"It was *s-o-o-o* my fault," she said.

"Impressionism gone wrong?" said the manager presenting wet cloths and complimentary refills.

Marguerite silently mourned. Was the stained jacket an omen?

"For the floor art," scowled a waitress arriving with paper towels, a bucket and mop.

Tepid toe squelch prompted Sidney to drop some of the paper towels to his splattered feet.

"Are those shoes what I think they are?" he asked.

"Long story," Marguerite replied.

"Not for the crocodile it wasn't!"

"Not an original statement."

"Do you think that's some sort of consolation to the beast?" he asked.

"The skins were a souvenir... courtesy of an ex... who killed the crocodile... that tried to eat him... on a golf course... in Africa."

Sidney raised his eyebrows. "You with him?"

"No," she said. "I don't do travel for pleasure."

"Boyfriend ever consider the croc might have been hungry?"

"Reptiles and you do deep and meaningful?" she asked.

"I can see why you dropped the boyfriend."

"At least the skin wasn't wasted."

"I prefer flip-flops... especially these gourmet enhanced ones," he said.

And so the meeting began. It was to be a joint project between two organisations from different ends of the spectrum. He crusaded. She campaigned. They both cared. He raised funds for a non-governmental organisation. It supported sustainable development that linked poor communities to global markets. She managed advertising strategies for FMG[3] retailers. They both worked too long, played too little and loved even less. It was a collision of collective enthusiasm for profit meets process... with all the frisson-sparked collaboration between polar-opposite consciences.

"Who have you chosen as the face for the advertisements?" she asked.

"His name is Urday," he said.

"Background?"

"He's sixteen... so I'm told."

"Photogenic?"

"Aren't they all at that age?"

"Depends – cherub or toe-rag? Angel or demon?"

"Not my area. I just want him to have a future."

"Speak any English?"

"Not really," he said, "but they worked with translators to make sure they got the truth."

"Whose version?"

"The version for our vision," he said.

"Ouch – sounds like a strap line," she laughed.

"I try hard. Our organisation's done lots of advertising campaigns for fair-trade products," he replied. "Urday works for a local entrepreneur. Makes designer flip-flops from re-cycled tyres."

---

[3] Fast moving consumer goods

"Sounds like an oxymoron," she said.

"You make me feel like one," he replied. "Well okay, they're flip-flops. Made from old rubber. The local women hand-paint the footwear. Designers in the West flog the finished product for inflated prices. Shorthand – they're designer flip-flops."

"That what you call those?" she said, surveying his footwear complete with sticky coffee-daubs.

They smiled at each other.

He warmed... a lot.

She melted... a little.

"Urday's entrepreneur got started through a micro-finance project," he began.

"Your organisation fund it?"

"We channelled the money. Seed funding was a donation from a multi-national."

"Who made their money how?" she asked.

"The parent company has lots of tentacles. Mainly known for its involvement with petrochemicals."

"Just gets better," she said with an edge. "Any recent scandals?"

"You mean like oil spills, environmental stuff ups?" he asked.

"Wider than that – worker exploitation, women's rights in the workforce, child labour issues, health and safety? Environmental scandals are only one small concern in the package."

"Not to our knowledge."

"We'll still have to downplay that petrochemical aspect," she said.

"The company say they're giving something back," he said.

"That has to stand up against a charge of grabbing the cake first, offering crumbs later," she replied.

"At least the company's at the table. Dialogue and action offer hope."

"You always dine with the devil?" she asked.

"That's good from someone with crocodile feet!"

She blushed... a little.

He bristled... a lot.

"We believe the boy Urday is healthy, works in light and well ventilated conditions, gets a fair wage for fair work," Sidney said.

"Who carried out the ethical checks?" Marguerite asked.

"Independent regulators," he said. "Using a quantifiable matrix on sustainable social economics. Ticks in the all the right boxes."

"When were the checks carried out?"

"The regulators went at the same time as the buyers," he explained.

"Tax efficient?"

"Hey I'm supposed to be the cynic," he replied.

"Did I say do-gooders had to be naïve?"

He smiled... to himself.

She smiled... to herself.

They looked at each other and smiled... a lot.

"Okay so we have the face for the fair trade campaign. Your organisation is satisfied that Urday is bone fide. I'm sure we can mount a major promotion within the budget to fit the target markets. But..."

"I knew there'd have to be a 'but'," he said.

"But I think it would be better to have two faces. Male and female. Fits both genders. Promotes equality... in addition to the primary objectives," she said.

"Shouldn't be a problem. I'm sure Urday has a sister or cousin or female friend that's photogenic."

"What about trans-cultural? To make it appeal to our politically correct sensitivities?" she said.

"Like you mean he wears a hoodie and she's in a hijab?"

"Not a bad idea," she said. "Might be a possibility. I'll need to do some market research on the possible impacts – positive and negative."

"How long will it take to finalise the campaign plan?" he asked.

"I should have a presentation ready with mock-up visuals and graphics within ten days," she said. "Shall we co-ordinate our diaries to see when both organisations can schedule a joint meeting? Your office or mine?"

"We do fair trade coffee," he winked.

"Lucky me," she replied.

When the date and presentation agenda were agreed, Sidney asked, "Will you use a local photographer?"

"Yes, of course" she replied. "Our agency holds a data bank."

"So, it won't be a problem?" he said.

"In fact I know the perfect candidate. Pandora, she's worked for us before."

"Good. Using a local will give the photographer an opportunity to access western markets for images."

"This photographer has worked in Europe as well as Africa. I'll check the legalities for rights and distribution."

"We could always travel there together – for the photo shoot. Might help if you saw the product first-hand?" he said.

She tensed.

Oh no... this was way too much... how to play this one?

He was puzzled.

Why had she changed? Perhaps the not-so-subtle innuendo was way too explicit?

He noticed how she gripped her hands – the knuckles were white.

She saw him notice.

They sat in silence.

"You know whether our boy Urday can customize those flip-flops?" she asked.

"Dare I ask why?"

"I hear crocodile trim is all the rage this season," she said.

"Isn't this where we started?" he asked. "You like flying close to the edge?"

"You've made the link!" she said.

"Sorry, I'm lost."

"Flying. Can't do the flying stuff with you," she said.

"Chicken," he replied. "I'm perfectly safe to travel with... seriously, I am. This banter's just a game... mostly. The work is for real... not a problem."

"It is a real problem. Not flirting. Flying, I mean. I'm scared of flying."

"Honestly?"

"Read the books, taken the pills, said the prayers," she said.

"And?" he asked.

"And... nothing works," she replied.

"You know fear and sexuality are linked?"

"That's the worst chat-up line I've ever heard," she said. "Do you know that vomit and vertigo rhyme with no way Jose?"

"A compromise? If you can't go to Urday, maybe he can come to us?"

He offered a solution... at least.

She reflected on it... at length.

They nodded in harmony... at last.

"Luck can link a dream to reality," he said.

"Maybe," she smiled. "So what are my chances of getting another carrot juice undiluted with cappuccino?"

Tee and Tort

I am Graham Gembell-Glast and I am an agoraphobic.

My virtual, cyber-link therapist tells me that keeping a written record will help – action to limit damages – tort and true. I'm also writing because my firm's insurance policy, clause 79.2, paragraph a(i) headed *Key Staff: discretionary extended leave of absence*, won't pay out if I don't comply with the rigorous conditions. In other words, do what you're told or you're screwed.

So, Therapist, here is a chapter in my story – earn your keep and give counsel on what you learn.

A summary of Graham Gembell-Glast would include:

- a solicitor and senior partner in a large London firm
- a golfer with a damn fine handicap of nine
- in robust physical health
- a fine palate for good food and new world wines
- heterosexual and constant
- single

I have yet to find a woman who meets the triple G checklist: geisha in the home, goddess in the bedroom, gem on the golf course. To date women in my life have scored two out of three but never a hat trick. Compromise is not an option. My legal experience indicates that compromise equals diminished rewards. Consequently there seems little point in substituting other G words – genteel, glamorous, giddy or downright ghastly – to affect a proposal. Single and searching is my motto. I apply my golf methods to my life – work and play – assess, action, appreciate, advance.

I've been a golfer since school, a solicitor since university, an agoraphobic since I went on holiday to Africa. I went with a client, a professional golfer turned celebrity sports writer. My firm represents his intellectual

33

property rights. He's become a friend despite our perspectives on life. Golf is his work whereas I work to play golf. He plays with women. They adore him. He dumps them when they get serious. Women to me are a serious study in time, motion and money. They like my money. They spend their time working on me to spend it on them. Women dump me when I get serious about balancing expenditure with benefits. Perhaps the Marguerite saga will have a different outcome... if I can ever get out of this bunker in which I now reside.

It wasn't the wilds of Africa that got to me. Nor the never-ending poverty that I encountered on that fateful trip. My agoraphobia started and ended when I saw a crocodile eat a child. Since then I've hatched every type of phobia possible, though I don't know the medical jargon. But whatever crocodile-phobia, golf-club phobia, hijab-phobia and quite possibly will-to-breathe-phobia are called, I've got them incubating big time. I haven't left my house for six months. Correction I haven't left my bedroom for six months. It's got four walls, a window with shutters, brocade curtains, a super-king sized bed, an en-suite with Jacuzzi, built-in wardrobes with mirror doors and internal lights, an OLED television, a telephone with broadband connected, a computer and a kettle. What else could an agoraphobic desire?

Every ten days my sister delivers a box of goodies – packets of soups (add boiling water and stir), sachets of flavoured drinks and chocolate biscuits (dunk and drink), bread sticks (Italian) and apples (Granny Smiths) – and takes out the rubbish.

She says, "This can't continue, Graham. You need help."

I say, "Why not? Who helped the kid? I'm safe here."

Sleeping is my major challenge. Hamlet had it to the tee

– *To be or not to be?* The question is futile. I would rather be asleep. Not be awake all night, every night. But the dilemma is, as the good bard's spokesman spouts, *To sleep: perchance to dream: ay, there's the rub; For in that sleep of death what dreams may come…*

Sometimes I just can't fall asleep. The head says no, the body screams yes. The eyelids are closer to the head. I no longer have the heart to argue. Other times I fall asleep and dream… the same nightmare… the crocodile, the child, the blood, the minced and splattered flesh… death dreams… snuff sleep.

To cope, I have devised a ritual. It heralds time to relax as opposed to work time. Order… steady progress… control… stealth comfort.

I walk twice around the bathroom forwards… and then backwards… left foot first. I take off my shirt. I turn on the tap. I put the plug in the bath. I take off my left sock. I get the soap from one end of the bath and put it at the other end… always sideways with the embossed, brand-sign face up. If the soap sign is worn, I throw the soap away. A new bar is unwrapped.

"What do you do with the soap?" my sister says. "Eat it?"

"Tastes like crocodile, I'm told."

"Stop it, that's enough," she shouts.

After that I remove my right sock, my vest, my trousers and finally my briefs. In that order and only in that order. No deviation permitted. Systems are what work. I know this from the office. I have never misplaced a legal document because I always follow exactly the same method. In thirty years that method has never failed.

Then I fold every item. Except the socks which I fold over their tops, precisely three centimetres, and bind together. The socks go into and out of the washing machine like that, never separated, never lost, forever coupled, a lasting pair.

My sister remains unconvinced that this course of action will heal me.

"You're a troubled soul, Graham. The ghosts must be laid to rest."

Well that leaves another triple G choice – God, ghost-buster or guru. As for the first, I'm not convinced that He's got my number. The second is as likely to be a charlatan as a champion. So I figure that I must make do with therapy-on-line.com cum mental guru.

That's you, my virtual therapist.

Washing down advice with some single malt whiskey is also remedial I find.

Marguerite rang a month after I got back. She said she needed my help. She didn't mention her ex… or our trip… or her fear of flying. No extraneous detail. Focus and forward. Does she play golf I wonder, or merely play with golfers?

"You know, Graham," my sister says, "the best thing to do when you fall off a horse is to get right back on."

"The croc didn't eat a horse," I say.

"I've got a client… linked to the sustainable development campaign… fair trade flip-flops… I need your help," Marguerite says softly over the phone.

"Not sure I'm the right person," I say.

"Graham, you write the textbooks on intellectual property. Who else is there?"

"You've got to put it behind you," my sister nags. "Start again. Maybe a group session would help? I read in one of those magazines that you can share your experiences with other survivors. Post-traumatic stress counselling they call it."

"How many people do you think there are who watch crocodiles eat kids?" I say.

"You can do it," she replies.

"Should I look under snuff movies for reptile lovers?"

"You can do it… for me?" Marguerite says again on the telephone. "Please."

"What do you want help with?" I ask.

"Graham, you're an angel. Thank you. Shall I come visit and talk it over?"

"No," I reply. "I don't do visitors."

"What about a… sort of friend?"

"Business and friends aren't a good deal at the moment," I say.

"I shall send an email to your retreat with all the details," she says. "And then we will talk. My place or yours, wherever you want."

"The zoo near the airport?" I say.

She pauses. "If you like. But I have to warn you now that I'm not brave."

"Me neither. We're perfectly matched."

She doesn't respond.

Her email arrives within twenty four hours. The crux of the matter concerns a photographer called Pandora. Marguerite is commissioning this indigenous photographer in Kenya to shoot stills for a campaign in Europe. How can the photographer's work be protected, exposure of it controlled, with benefits accruing to the artist? This is too easy. Marguerite will know the answers. She is a seasoned professional. I suspect her motives – caring or calculating? I would like to be wrong.

I walk to the bath. The ten step programme to recovery and relaxation begins again. Clean and clothed, I walk to my bed, draw back the three hundred thread cotton sheets, ease myself exactly half a metre from the left-hand bed edge and lie on my back – rigid – hands clasped. I recite Hamlet's soliloquy… forwards… and then backwards. To be asleep? Perchance to dream the nightmare?

Suddenly I roll from the bed, stride out of the bedroom, jump down the stairs, wrench open the door and jog out of the house. I see Marguerite waiting in my car. Her long, red hair cascades over her shoulders. The car engine hums. I approach the car door. Then I espy her foot, clad in crocodile-skin sandals, poised over the accelerator.

I… I turn back. It is too soon…

I wake up, heart racing, sweating, sit up and face myself in those mirrored doors.

I am Graham Gembell-Glast, golfer, solicitor, dreamer… and coward.

Check-in and Clock-off

"Did you pack this bag yourself? Has anyone asked you to carry anything for them in your bag? Could anyone have interfered with your bag at any time since you packed it?" Sinitta goes through the motions... blah, blah, blah.

Sooner or later everyone you know checks in at the airport – old friends, new enemies, ex-lovers, the famous face, a family member. Face to face with an impatient audience, Sinitta performs her repertoire to the queue with a plastered smile, a pretend interest in the all-look-the-same-customer, inane chit chat about the weather, choice of seat, schedule delays. Another day, another demand, another delivery.

"Are you okay?" her colleague asks.

"My back aches," Sinitta admits.

"You look... poorly."

"Not likely," Sinitta says and struggles with her smile. Her hand trembles on the computer. She pulls a tissue from her pocket and mops her face. Is this a signal? Her colleagues note her next passenger. They all have a sign for a really special one who has crossed their path and is to receive a treat resolution to match. Last time, Sinatra's quarry was Dirk, the hairdresser from hell. She had booked in for a treatment to give her hair a 'je ne sais quoi'. The hairdresser was supposed to lowlight and twirl the greying locks. She would blossom into a fair goddess. Instead she skulked out as a reject look-a-like from *Night of the Ghouls*. She said it took three months' salary and an Everest of conditioner to fix that spiral perm, bleached beyond follicle recovery. Dirk didn't recognise the pleasant smile of the home-dyed, block brunette behind the check-in counter. But Sinitta remembered Dirk. He got assigned the special seat – next to the loo, surrounded by a cheerleading team of pubescent girls, drowning in cheap perfumes and gelled hair sculptures, giggling with verbal diarrhoea – for his seven hour flight.

"Made my day!" she said.

The staff want to make today special for Sinitta. It is her last day of work at this airport – forty years of service off and on. Mostly on with the obligatory time off for breeding (maternity leave was hard fought in those early days), healing (all those colds and sneezes caught from passengers and public places), and the odd leaving (code for mental health days when you just can't face another whining passenger without resorting to physical violence). It's also Sinitta's birthday. At 16:00 she officially becomes a pumpkin.

"You want to clock off a bit early?" someone asks her.

"Won't say no," Sinitta replies. She starts to say something. It sounds blurred. She licks her lips, grips the desk and breathes slowly.

"What's up?" someone asks.

"D-day, that's all," Sinitta replies in her low voice. "Maybe it'll be a dead-darling day after all."

We look blank. When she sees their puzzled looks, she explains.

"My niece, Nala, calls them dead-darling days in her village in Africa. Family story – have a birthday, drop dead."

"Don't even joke about it," her colleague says.

The staff are reminded of their supervisor who retired last year. Three months of uninterrupted gardening-by-numbers climaxed with a Christmas coronary and a wake fuelled with mulled wine and mini-mince pies.

"Maybe you can go visit that Nala niece of yours, in her far away land?"

"Maybe," she agrees and mops her face again.

The final clients of her career-in-closure step up to the check-in desk. The woman is nervous with a name to match – Marguerite – a half-breathless sibilant exotic, dressed in chi-chi travel comfort. The man is called Sidney – nonchalantly supportive in that laid-back, overly polite, pallid kind of English way.

"Any chance of an aisle seat?" he asks.

"Any special reason for the request?"

"She's not a brave flyer," he explains and clasps the woman's hand to his heart.

"Air travel is the safest form of transport."

"No choice," the nervous woman mutters. "Urday can't get a passport."

Sinitta wonders who the hell Urday is.

"Long story," Sidney says apologetically. "You don't want to know."

He's right. Sinitta doesn't. She hands them their boarding passes. The pair shuffle off towards the departure gate with its joys of immigration and air-side over-priced, under-powered coffee bars and tasteless duty-free shopping. Well, to be precise, Sidney shuffles and Marguerite hangs on for the ride.

"My fingers really tingle, tiptoes to shoulder," Sinitta says and logs off for the last time.

"Your hands are clammy," says her manager, shaking her hand goodbye. Such is the company legacy – no praise to the last.

Her colleagues expect to see a euphoric gesture, something, anything but... there is nothing. Sinitta leaves the counter with her handbag and security pass that will expire in sixty minutes. A colleague shouts her name. She turns, wan and sallow. Some of the staff are taking her out for farewell drinks.

"Go wait in my car," the colleague says. "It's unlocked."

Sinitta walks in the direction of the staff car park where she knows the security guard will be asleep. She looks for the colleague's blue car. There are two parked together. She is not sure which blue car is which. She chooses the one with the yellow toy elephant on the floor. She knows her workmate has a young son. She opens the back door and sinks into the seat. She closes her eyes and lists her top ten moments at the airport. Farting as she checked in the Prime Minister probably doesn't count but it makes her smile.

Sinitta becomes aware of people. A woman is sitting in the front seat of the car. Where did she come from? She hears the woman ask, "Are you scared?"

She does not know these people. Are they talking to her?

"No," a young man replies, "not if it's quick. Are you?"

"I'm not sure scared is the most appropriate terminology," the woman says.

"Academics – you love words," the man replies.

"They're toys," the woman says. "If you choose to play the game, you need the tools."

Sinitta wonders how long she has been dozing on the back seat. She puts the yellow toy elephant down and tries to sit up. Her arm won't move.

"Do you think they will be angry with us? For choosing this way?" the man asks.

"Some will. But we all have to make our own decisions on the things we believe to be important," the woman replies.

"Excuse me," Sinitta tries to say, "I am supposed to be having farewell drinks."

But they don't hear her. She can hear words inside her head. Have they travelled out her mouth? She wonders if these people are deaf or blind. Or is she dreaming some terrible retirement script? Have her colleagues arranged a nightmare prank – the retirement equivalent of a hen night stripper? Trapped in an academic debate? Relegated to death by Mastermind?

"I'm glad you think it's important that we die together," the man says.

"What could be more important?" the woman asks.

"Living longer."

"Perhaps dying together is living best," the woman replies.

"Such wise words," he smiles. "Is that the hypothesis your work supports?"

"No," the woman says." Different cultures have different rituals for death and grieving."

"So I read in your publications."

"Which one did you find the most interesting?"

"The one on transition from the living to the dead," the man says.

"Why did you like that one? It is not one of my more respected pieces."

"I liked the image that you posited about a space between living and dying – for both the living and the dying to reflect," the man replies.

"I've always wondered if there will be a short space between the two worlds," the woman says. "If in that space you are aware that it's over. The medics say that you don't feel pain when trauma actually occurs. It's a short time later, nano-seconds, maybe, that the mind allows the effects – the pain of the pulped body – to trickle into your consciousness."

"Like when you eat a sausage at a barbecue and the marinade dribbles down the fork onto your hand? You notice the sludge after it's started to flow."

"Ughhh," Sinitta grunts. This time she is sure that the sound has spewed from inside her head.

"Perhaps… although that's not quite the metaphor I would have chosen," the woman says.

"Wise words are wasted in times of intense doing."

"Ready?" the woman asks. She grinds the accelerator to the floor, revs the engine to fever scream. He places his hand on hers. They grip the juddering hand brake, bodies primed and pumping.

"Ughhh," Sinitta repeats from the back seat. "Help… help, please."

The man and the woman look around. They see Sinitta, a middle-aged, stroke-silent, frothing sack diagonally slumped with a yellow elephant half-gripped in a frozen hand. Startled, they forget to hold the brake. The car bucks and charges… full throttle… towards the concrete pylon. Six eyes stare at each other, a disparate coven of estranged hearts… in full flight for the hereafter.

Sinatra's colleagues noted that the staff newsletter carried a three line statement of regret. A former employee had tragically lost her life. No compensation will be paid to her family. Sinitta was off duty and recently retired.

Her friends read the headlines in local paper: "Stroke victim in suicide speed pact."

The coroner's report recorded accidental death.

Is that what clocking-off after sixty years of breathing and forty years as a national airline employee is worth… blah… blah… blah?

44

Whales and Words

My friend Jonah is a Mzungu, a white person... but I like him anyway.

"Urday," he says, "want to learn something new?"

Jonah tells me all sorts of stories, some of them true stuff. Some of them maybe not really true... but they make me laugh. My friend Nala says Jonah is a living library. He told us that he was named after Whale. Whale was a big fish. The big fish swallowed Jonah. Then three days later Whale spat him out. Nala and I double wink and nod, polite-like, to his face.

As if!

Mzungus, but not Jonah, act really weird around us locals. They shout in slow motion.

"DO-YOU-KNOW-THE-WAY-TO-THE...
wherever?"

Is this because foreigners think we local kids have fog brains? In our culture we don't talk down to people who do not have good fortune. So we kids nod... extra slowly... back at the Mzungu. Sometimes we play the not so nice game. Like when they ask, "WHERE-CAN-I-GET-WATER?"

We pretend not to understand. We point and slow speak their question back to them.

"Can-get-water-yes?"

Then we send them to the public toilet. We locals need a good laugh too.

Mzungus speak to their own in foreign-folk-kind talk. Which we kids get even though foreigners think we don't understand. About stuff that foreigners find interesting... like sex.

"Ignorance isn't it?" they say. "Shame – all those kids!"
What a laugh!

45

How do those foreigners think my parents got all us kids? Not spat out of big fish, that's for sure. Us kids don't talk about sex... in front of foreigners... but we know about it. Do Mzungus talk in front of their kids about their parents having sex? Nala's uncle reckons foreigners would 'cause they treat their parents like shit. One of the flip-flop buyers who came to my factory boasted about sending his father away to live in a house with other old people. The Mzungu's old dad didn't even know the other old people he had to share the house with.

How weird is that?

The Mzungu told the story to Nala's uncle when they were playing golf. You give your dad away and brag about it to a stranger when you are playing a game. Foreigners might be rich but kind they are not.

Nala thinks Jonah might tell me the truth about the whale-sex-birth story when she is not around. Now that Nala wears a hijab she says that it's the end of story time with Jonah for her.

"Maybe not," I say, "'cause Jonah's different."

"He's still Mzungu. He's still a whitey."

"Not in Jonah's world," I say. "Everyone is black."

Before hijab, Nala was allowed to be around Jonah 'cause Nala was invisible. Not like that character in Jonah's foreign story. That invisible man wore bandages so people wouldn't walk into him. If that was me I would wear bright clothes that smelt bad. Then everyone would avoid me.

"Nala," I explain, "you are more than a voice. Like me, only different, kind of. You're a girl voice."

Jonah says he can see voices though his ears. True, he does, no lies, special Mzungu ears. And for sure, he can tell straight away if Nala and me are smiling at what he says.

Weird and wonderful!

Maybe Jonah is blind 'cause of something to do with

big fish spit? Like when a snake shoots poison into dog eyes. Nala says it's not polite to ask. Nala's uncle says a blind man is a warning from the gods.

"Don't look on an evil eye," he warns.

Nala's mum says Uncle is arse-talking rubbish.

"Allah," she says, "has a reason for making a man blind. Accept and be kind."

All Nala and me know is that Jonah is blind but he doesn't act blind. We would like to ask him about evil eyes but then I guess he would guess why we wanted to know. So we don't.

A few days ago me and Jonah went fishing. We catch lots of things – old shoes but never a pair, half a bus tyre, dead dog legs, and once a bangle that sparkled. Never fish, not live ones anyway. I once asked Jonah if the water from the flip-flop factory makes the fish sick.

"Good hypothesis Urday," Jonah replied. "Now you have to prove it."

Once Nala and me caught a glass box. Inside it there was the biggest fish I had even seen. Dead it was, and stuck to the wall of the glass box. One part of the glass wall was cracked so me and Nala tapped out the broken chips to let Jonah feel the contents but not cut his hands. We were so excited.

"Small fry," Jonah pronounced.

"I thought it might be Whale," Nala said.

"There is not a box big enough to put a whale inside," said Jonah.

Nala looked at me. I double winked at her. That's our sign not to disagree in case we upset Jonah. Nala double winked back.

"Winking won't change the truth," said Jonah.

We didn't say anything or even wink. But I knew Nala was thinking about the giant metal box that had arrived at my factory. Thousands of pairs of flip-flops could fit inside that box when it was shipped to foreign places. Surely Whale couldn't be bigger than that?

"Got news Urday?" Jonah said, casting his line into the river.

"Not me but Nala has," I say.

"Good or bad?"

"That depends," I say, quite unsure of what the value of the verdict should be. "Nala has another notch on her dead-darling-day post."

"Whose birthday then? A close relation?" Jonah asks.

"Not really. Her Aunty Sinitta got deaded."

"How?" asks Jonah.

"Car crash in England," I say.

"How's that for a chocolate frog?" Jonah says. "Ugly, so did a friend of mine."

I do not know how to answer this. Our frogs are not made of chocolate. They are ugly though. I say nothing.

"Very messy car crash... double suicide... with her son... her illegitimate son," continues Jonah.

Jonah's friends are living soap operas... suicide... illegitimate... better stories than television.

"They want to bring Aunty Sinatra's body home?"

Jonah understands our ways.

"It'll cost," says Jonah.

"What will happen to your friend and her bastard?" I ask.

"Not sure," Jonah says. "Her husband didn't know."

How can a husband not know his wife had a baby with another man?

How can a wife have a baby with another man and not be punished?

"Is the husband of the dead wife blind?" I ask.

"Not in that way," says Jonah. "Maybe he turned a blind eye... under the circumstances."

Blind eye, evil eye, Mzungu ways of seeing.

Now I understand what Jonah means when he says, "It's all Greek to me." Even though his friend lives in England.

"You and Nala ready for the foreigners?" Jonah asks.

"Nala's uncle has agreed," I say.

"That photo shoot is worth a mountain of money."

"Nala's mother says you can't eat money," I say.

"What do you think Urday?" Jonah asks.

"True what Nala's mum said… but it can buy a lot of chapatti flour and maybe a good funeral for dead Aunty Sinitta."

"Urday, you're a wise old boy."

"Wisdom comes with age. I learn from my elders."

"Shall I tell you something not so wise?" asks Jonah.

"Sure," I say. "Is it a true story? Or a message story with not so true stuff?"

Jonah turns his head towards me.

"My friend, the one in the car crash," Jonah begins, "I worked with her once, out here. We were students, anthropologists, playing at field work. She dumped me, flew home, got her doctorate, became a professor, got married, had a baby girl. Was supposed to live happily ever after."

Not so happy if she was in a hurry to get to the hereafter.

"Me, I came back here. Wanted to keep on with my field research. She said to me when we parted, 'Jonah, remember Africa is the shape of a human heart. The wilderness myths will pump your blood, self-invention will pound your brain.'"

"I don't understand her words," I say.

"She meant that I could leave Africa but it would never leave me."

Nala's mother makes more sense than Mzungu professors.

"Do you think all the people who die on the same day go to meet their god together?" I ask.

"Like catching the bus – destination express to heaven? Board here, same price ticket, all zones, all day?" Jonah asks.

I do not know how to reply.

"Good question, Urday. No answer."

"What would your dead friend say?" I ask.

"That depends," replies Jonah.

"On what factors?" I enquire. "Is this a maths question about probability?"

I love maths. Jonah tells me I would come top of the class at Mzungu school.

"Sort of. The probability is shaped by how much she drank," Jonah says, "and which old fart of a professor or young student she wanted to impress. She could play an audience to eat out of her hand."

Mzungu ways and manners shock Nala and me. Why would any person want to eat from the hand of another? Like a master feeding his dog. A professor who farts, a teacher who flirts with students – foreign classrooms are not like mine. This maths question is harder than I thought. What has the volume of liquid consumed got to do with thinking and talking? The problem must be about logic, not probability.

"It seems to me," I say to Jonah, "that if a university education means drinking alcohol, bastard children and suicide driving – well that is not necessarily my wish for graduation."

"Ah Urday," replies Jonah, "life and love cannot be learned. Remember, my young guru, that it is probably better to ask for forgiveness than permission."

Pixels and Pandora

"Je t'adore, Pandor… rrrra! Je t'adore, Pandor… rrrra," her dada would chant on a Thursday evening, the servants' night off. He liked to wear a pink polka dot apron whilst stirring his infamous tomato ragout. Her dada… kitchen philosopher, cook and storyteller… who persuaded her mama that Pandora was a proper name. He was a French-speaking, Greek doctor with a mission to reduce infant mortality; a huge, hairy and garlic-passioned man. Her mama was a local nurse with lustrous ebony skin, gusting with love, whirling with dance and singing delight. It was a game of musical doctors and nurses… before, during and after hours. The spawn of their union became a local legend… the mulatto of Mombasa… Pandora. His naming gift for her was a wooden box, carved from the entrails of a sunken dhow, a spice boat from Zanzibar, in which the spoils of knowledge were gathered to provide fodder for the child's intellect.

When she was eight Pandora announced that the legend was true. She found her precious box open. The words of wisdom were still there, poignant and glistening, but the evils had winged it. She was cursed. Her mother had died the week before from malaria. There was no hope.

Father and daughter moved from their large house beside the beach to a small apartment close to the hospital where he worked. The doctor stopped cooking. He stopped giving her cards with wise words. He closed her wooden box. He put the box in a cupboard. Instead of chants and songs he quoted Nietzsche, a name that sounded like bitter medicine.

"For women," the doctor would say, "a man is the means; the end is always a child."

Did this mean he loved or loathed her?

Her adored dada abandoned her two years later. After his funeral her ayah explained, "He who has health has hope; he who has hope has everything."

Pandora wrote down the adage, recovered the box and filed the words under medicine. At the time she took it to mean that she would have to go live with Mr Healthy – her dada's name for the hospital security guard, a fat man with no teeth and four wives. She was relieved to find the saying was only an Arabian proverb.

Being a mixed race orphan in Africa with the name of Pandora had its challenges. Her name might mean hope. But her experience was quite the opposite. Where was the link with her expectation and desire?

An Aunt Alexis arrived from Grenoble via Athens to collect the inheritance and the chattels. An elegant, statuesque musician of indeterminate age, the aunt had left the family pile in Greece, spent a fortune with her plastic surgeon and hairdresser to ensure a metamorphosis from hook nose to button cute and brunette frizz to blond sheen. Aunt Alexis had married an aging French academic who kept her fed, watered and at a distance while he played with old texts and young testicles. The inheritance was substantial and welcome. The chattels – the child and her suitcase with its magic box full of the wise words of others – were more problematic. A ten year old émigré is too young to be left alone but far too old to be seen as a designer accessory. Part of the inheritance went to her boarding school in Switzerland. The remainder her aunt spent on school holidays, avoiding her. At thirteen Pandora had been round the world twice, knew a Chablis from a Chardonnay, swore in eleven languages and collected seven hideous rosettes for the annual school art prize. She was alone and lonely, nicknamed 'the half caste from Hades' by her fellow students.

At eighteen Pandora announced her plan to be a trapeze artist at a nightclub in Paris. Aunty Alexis sent a cheque for 10,000 francs and a card saying 'Some see a hopeless end, while others see an endless hope.'

Pandora filed the card under optimism and bought a one way ticket to Paris. She never made it as a trapeze artist, but a can-can dancer gave her a camera as a birthday consolation. By twenty four she was earning a living as a photographer in a city where she spoke the language but never belonged. An exotic in a cage – always looking out, capturing images of life while only half-living herself. She inhaled with hope, exhaled in lethargy.

And then life offered a variety of Margarita.

"Pandora of the pixels," Marguerite announced, when she found herself sharing accommodation in the proverbial turret in the eighteenth arrondissement. Red haired Marguerite was a writer from London. Coffee coloured Pandora was shutter-clicking in Paris. They were wanton women together experiencing the pleasures that only a rite of passage can offer… without the wisdom of achievement, the cynicism of experience, the exhaustion of fulfilment. The world and everyone's husband loved Marguerite. She found men to be available, expendable and insubstantial – like tissues. Pandora was her shadow – the tawny pearl flanking the garnet-haired nymph – her first real friend.

By the time Pandora had deciphered the true meaning of her sisterhood spell, Marguerite was off to New York via London, Delhi, Sydney and the Cook Islands for the adventure that became her career. Letters, faxes and emails traced her meteoric professional success and mapped her personal escapades in love and lust. Pandora kept the best pieces of correspondence, filed under essence.

On a lonely night, when work or play is not to her taste she opens the box to find pleasure in the snippets.

Technically, Pandora is a thirty-nine-year-old virgin, Marguerite's nemesis, the goddess of retribution for unrequited love. Metaphorically she is the adjectival slag, the epitome of courtly love – to pine but never to deliver, to adore but not to sally, to cherish but not to spoil. Her fondest image of the Parisian sojourn sits in a mother-of-pearl frame. It is a self-portrait in sepia of the two young women. In the photograph Pandora and Marguerite are sprawled across a sofa. In the background a dormer window shows rain falling on old roof tiles. There is a low fire to the side in the foreground. Marguerite is posed reading a book. The book is a pock-marked, leather-bound volume of Shakespeare's sonnets, in English. Pandora had uncovered the edition at a flea market below Sacre Coeur. The image stirs memories for her – the beauty of the rhythms, the images of grace, the stories of love lost and located, of torturous games and lofty prizes, of food and fortitude. Pandora drank those evenings and ate their worth. Those days were gifts for her tomorrows.

Marguerite's emails of late are not so pithy or full of detail but clearly Marguerite is still Marguerite. The world waits upon her. She tells Pandora of a man called Sidney.

> *Have completed yet another fear of flying course. Can't believe that I have agreed to fly all the way to Kenya for work! Sidney promises to hold my hand – poor fool him. He may change his mind after I've upchucked half way across the Indian Ocean. Do planes carry a bottomless stash of sick bags?*

Pandora asks her if Sidney is a saint or the latest sinner. She smiles at Marguerite's reply.

Pandora,

Honestly, Sidney is a male. Obvious good points. Enjoys playing Adam and Eve. Some very irritating traits. Not connected to apples. For how long? Answers on a postcard?

Pandora has some sympathy for this Sidney man with whom Marguerite toys. And then there is Graham, mad and sad. His ploy with Marguerite is foiled.

Have spoken to my contact Graham Gembell-Glast about intellectual property rights re your photographs for the global campaign. Will bring his written advice for you to consider. You owe me woman – he is bright but. Still sorting mental health issues from his trip to Africa with my golfing ex. Nothing wrong with his libido. Men who needs them?

Pandora's correspondence to Marguerite is filled with background facts about her subjects for the photo shoot.

Darling Marguerite,

You will adore Urday and Nala. He's cute and she's drop dead gorgeous with a mischievous twinkle. I think the Imam has his hands full trying to keep her under wraps. Imagine Bambi meets Tinkerbelle under the gaze of Zeus.

The youngsters have hatched a plot to marry me off – exotica and the Englishman they presume. They're trying to match-make me with an ex-pat. He's a middle aged, blind anthropologist who's gone tropo in Africa. His name's Jonah and the

kids believe he's whale vomit. Pretty meets
gritty? Need I say more?

Marguerite replies, voicing concern over Pandora's
reference to the Imam. Is Pandora into mosques? Has she
found love on the road to Damascus or the dunes of Mecca?
Pandora assures that she still drinks the Bailey's concoction
Marguerite fed her in Paris and writes:

Darling Marguerite,

*No church, no mosque, no love. I don't need the
first two. I live in hope for the last. I'm not called
Pandora for nothing.*

She is reminded of her dada sprouting Nietzsche:
"There are no facts, only interpretations."

The Raw and the Cooked

A blind academic may see no evil. That does not mean that he thinks no evil or hears no evil.

I know all the protagonists. I sense their intention, smell their action and taste their expectation. The world might discard the less perfect, blank the disabled and ignore the peripheral. But a blind man neither discounts his own vulnerabilities nor dismisses the power of his lop-sided senses. The bat, blind as, avoids the tree. If only the able-sighted could remember that a damaged body is not disembodied.

"Jonah," asks Urday, "did you know that the photographer is a Greek goddess?"

"I thought goddesses were white people like you," adds says Nala.

Mmm, methinks Afro-Chinese whispers fall somewhere between reality and perception.

"Tell me what the woman said," I ask.

"She said her name is Pandora. Hope is her fame and photography her game," repeats Urday.

"Is she a famous Greek?" asks Nala.

"Is she a winner in those Greek games you told us about?" asks Urday.

"The Olympics?"

I try to explain the myth and the context of this Pandora's mixed race background with her Greek dad and Kenyan mum. The teenagers are satisfied.

"Is there a Marguerite legend too?" asks Nala.

"Not that I know of," I reply. "It's just a beautiful French name."

"It suits her," says Urday.

"What does she look like?" I ask the youngsters.

"Skinny with red hair," says Urday.

"She looks like an angel," says Nala. "Her skin is like that statue of William Shakespeare you have on your writing desk."

"Alabaster?"

"Exactly," says Nala, "and she has long red hair, sort of curly but not so tight like me and Urday."

"Wavy hair? How long?"

"It's hard to say. She usually has it piled up on top of her head. Too hot I think to leave it down. I think she looks like an angel."

"Why?"

"When she stands in front of the sun, it lights up like those pictures you see in Mzungu books."

"You've been spying on her Nala," says Urday.

"I've never seen anyone so beautiful in my whole life. I like looking at her," admits Nala shyly.

"I like listening to Marguerite," I say. I cannot tell them how I have been seduced by the erotic cadence of her voice. I am aroused – the voice and the vision are perfectly tuned.

"She might know about Whale," suggests Urday.

"No," says Nala. "Jonah just told us the French don't have legends. But Pandora will know."

Oh no, a conspiracy is hatching. I shake my head with mild despair. I have no romantic interest in Pandora. From her conversation with others, I suspect men are not her quarry. I know we share a common soft spot for Marguerite; she from a long ago experience in a world away from Kenya; me with unrequited interest. For Nala and Urday the uncharted territory of alternative sexualities is right up there with whale vomit and the story of my biblical namesake.

Perched on the sidelines, time ticking, vacillating from freak show to confidante to participant observer, I dictate my field notes to memory. Old habits resist change. It is Ramadan and the village is short-fused with too little carbohydrate and too long a wait before the call to prayer. The foreigners, Sidney and Marguerite, are tense-tired in the steamy heat. The photo shoot has long over run... again. Pandora, the photographer, is not satisfied... still. The atmosphere is mutinous with simmering hunger, festering hormones and volcanic exhaustion.

Anthropologists like me have spent years in Africa trying to extrapolate theories of kinship from group dynamics. Our diaries are full of charts that link a woman from this tribe to that village behaviour. Hypotheses are the stuff of higher research. My African friends have little need for elaborate academic dissertations. They know who they are and to what they are connected. It is me, the Mzungu observer, who tries to make sense of my identity and link it with place and name. I have travelled far to study myself. We foreigners wonder at what we uncover. Yet it is ourselves, the eternal outsider, who we contemplate.

This week, sitting beside the group, eavesdropping, I listen to Urday investigating his new topic. He tackles Pandora about tourism. In his world the tourist is an icon... to be observed, to envy, to long to be.

"I want to be a tourist when I grow up."

"Why?" she asks.

"Tourists are rich. They don't work. They play all the time. They eat and drink whenever they want," he tells her earnestly.

"Possibly," agrees Pandora, "but probably only when they are on holiday."

"Their life is one long holiday."

"Not for most of them Urday," she says. "They work all year at their jobs. They work in factories, schools, hospitals and offices. They have to work to come on holiday. They save their money and come here to play."

"True?" asks Urday.

"Yes," states Pandora. "They're rich by your village standards. But not in their own country. They couldn't pay school fees for one of their children on what your uncle earns."

"You sure about that?"

"Yes," says Pandora. "They play hard here. They work hard there."

I follow my protégé's progress with greedy pleasure. He is surely my little professor in the making. I anticipate a grilling on the economics of tourism by Urday later in the week.

Nala is fascinated by Pandora. It is the first time she has encountered a third space with something of one side mixed with the other. Pandora is mixed race, a permanently tanned woman with a white name, a Muslim who earns her living with a camera. Forbidden and fantastic, the exotic and the damned.

"What about what the Imam says?" Nala asks. "Muslims don't take images of other people."

"I choose to keep away from Imams," Pandora says.

"Must be good to be a grown up," muses Nala.

"Has its uses," agrees Pandora. "I like to think my work helps people. I can link people here with a world out there. Not all worlds listen to an Imam."

"Wicked," exclaims Nala, demonstrating the language impact of foreign radio programmes. "Is that what all Mzungu think?"

"It's not as simple as that. Lots of people – so lots of different ideas."

"Like what?" asks Nala.

"Well some foreigners like to travel with a camera and take pictures of people at places they visit. When they go home they can look at the images. That brings back all the happy memories of their trip. But others don't agree."

"Like who?" asks Nala.

"Like the Nubians."

"The Nubians – as in Africa Nubians?"

"Yes," replies Pandora. "When I was there, the Nubians didn't like having their photographs taken. They got angry with cameras."

"Didn't the tourists pay them money?" said Nala.

"Money wasn't the problem. The tourists offered to pay. The village elders said no and asked them to leave," replied Pandora.

"No kidding? Turning down money!"

"Money was not as precious to them as their privacy."

"Did the tourists get cross?"

"They didn't really get it," said Pandora. "The Nubians were really puzzled."

"Why?"

"They wanted me to tell them what was wrong. Why would foreigners want to leave their own home and go visit a stranger's house?" explained Pandora.

Nala said to Pandora, "So it was kind of all Greek to them?" and they both laughed.

Three days ago my prize for chief confidante put me at the centre of the edge. It was sunset and the day's shoot had finished. My young protégées were excited and keen to go to their village.

"True story Jonah," Urday said. "We're going to fly across the sea to England."

I smelt Marguerite's muskiness as she approached and asked me to join her for a sun-downer. I played my trump card.

"Take my arm and lead me up the garden path," I said. She giggled softly. I imagined how the intimacy of the evening might develop.

Two or three cold beers later she asked for my opinion.

61

She did not really want my take on her plan, merely an affirmation. I was repelled by my negative thoughts.

"My company has agreed to sponsor Nala's education."

"Here?" I asked.

"No, there, in England."

Poverty is hard to define but easy to smell. I knew what she was offering was generous and kind. I hated that her gift would bankrupt my emotional reserves. She may not have noticed Jonah the man but the link between Nala, Urday and me is almost umbilical. To share our travel tales but not share a seat? Will it be enough? Can there ever be enough?

"The girl is bright and keen. It's a great opportunity don't you think?" Marguerite continued.

"You want me to say that I think it's a great idea for Nala to become one of the international Diaspora? Forever away from home yet never able to leave the home of her heart... like your friend Pandora?"

"Nala will be able to enter a world beyond the hijab of her village," replied Marguerite.

"Nala lives in a world of absolutes and binary opposites, the poor and the privileged, black and white, men and women, raw and cooked."

Marguerite took my hand and fell silent.

"And Urday? What have you got planned for him? There is a plan, isn't there?"

I did not remove my hand. Blind beggars do not choose to reject warmth.

"My ex-boyfriend has arranged a scholarship to one of the best schools in Britain," she said.

"Urday will play golf with the privileged while he studies with the best?"

I stopped listening. Silence screamed in the waves and wallows of yearning and mourning.

"What do you think?" she asked.

"About which bit?"

"The wallet?" Marguerite said.

"Sorry, say that bit again."

"My ex had a wallet made from the crocodile skin. He wants me to give it to Urday. It's to be a souvenir of his bravery. I'm not sure. Sidney thinks it beyond horrendous. What do you think?"

If Sidney disagreed I wanted to shout, "It's a great idea!"

"Urday would certainly place it right up there with his school prizes. His family would be honoured. But Nala might not see it that way," I replied. "It was her sister that the crocodile ate."

"Ah love's young dream," Marguerite said.

"That's not how they see themselves."

"No, not yet," agreed Marguerite. "Love sometimes just sits dozing, not knowing when it might bloom."

Like Pandora in her dark room? A life, half exposed? Heart Noir?

Tonight Marguerite, her arm through mine, walks me to dinner.

"The last supper," I say.

"A celebration for friends, old and new," she replies.

Sidney and I are privy to tales of the past exploits of Pandora and Marguerite. I listen. I learn. The women shared a flat in Paris, starting careers, tasting life, fast and furious in their appetites. Is there something in Pandora's voice that suggests her memories of sharing are still tender? It clearly sounds like archive material when Marguerite describes the time. Sidney asks questions. He is naïve. The women's past belies his future.

"I'm hopeful that something will blossom when Pandora meets Graham. He's a colleague of Marguerite's," he confides when the women leave the table for a time.

How can he be so autistic in his miscomprehension of the dynamics?

"You don't think that this lawyer, Graham what's his name, fancies Marguerite?"

Sidney says nothing. I enjoy his discomfort. No doubt Graham is delighted to advise any friend of Marguerite's on intellectual property rights. Knowledge is his chosen tool of seduction – of Marguerite.

"Well it's my professional good luck to work with Marguerite during the day and dally with her after dark," Sidney replies.

"Back to London tomorrow then? Big wide world again?"

"You'll miss us all Jonah," he says.

"Too true."

"You ever thought of getting a guide dog or something?"

"Are you blind Sidney? I don't need one. All this is familiar."

"Marguerite will be devastated to know her arm-in-arms with you were unnecessary," says Sidney.

Touché.

Marguerite goes tomorrow. Back to London, holding his hand to quiet her fear of flying. She will collect the air miles and donate them to Urday and Nala, enabling the youngsters to return home on holidays. I will share the crumbs of their adventures.

But tonight in my dreams, where lust is layered with love, and Goliath and David fence with weapons of language and principles, I will thwart my rival Sidney and deconstruct our eternal triangle. Can the whale ignore Jonah? How does a blind man envisage a miracle? Will the links in our lives, forged with contradictions, continue to shape, support and separate us? As I say farewell to Sidney and Marguerite, standing chicken-like beside Pandora, Urday and Nala, I am reminded of the words of Francis Bacon: "Like the wisdom of crocodiles that shed tears when they would devour."

DRAMATIC LINKS

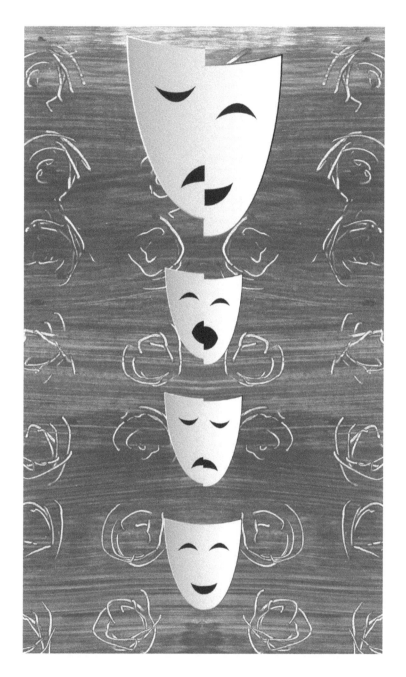

Wyeway Village Annual Pantomime

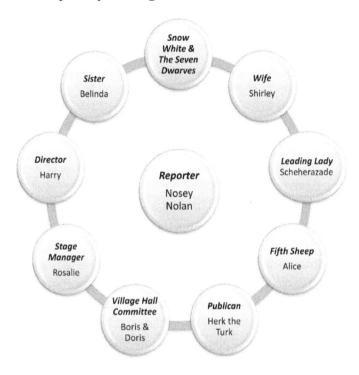

Snow White & The Seven Dwarves

Sister
Belinda

Wife
Shirley

Director
Harry

Reporter
Nosey Nolan

Leading Lady
Scheherazade

Stage Manager
Rosalie

Fifth Sheep
Alice

Village Hall Committee
Boris & Doris

Publican
Herk the Turk

The County Chronicle
News and views on what's happening locally

Professor returns from the land down under

The village of Wyeway is celebrating the return of its most famous academic export. After seven years in Australia, Professor Godfrey Nolan was guest of honour at a welcome home party held at the Turkey and Tree.

Nolan's sister, Mrs Belinda Prince, wife of one of television's best known soap opera stars, hosted seventy people on Saturday evening.

"It's wonderful having my brother around again," she said. "Skyping and emailing just isn't the same."

Many of Nolan's guests had followed his time in Australia via his blog. This year he will write a guest feature for this paper on the annual pantomime. Entitled *Snow White and the Seven Dwarves*, the script has been devised by Belinda.

Professor Nolan lived and worked in Toowoomba, a large country town in Queensland, 700 metres above sea level, known for its annual flower festival. In 2011 the town acquired an international reputation when it was devastated by an inland tsunami.

An exhibition of Nolan's photographs taken in Australia will be on display in the Wyeway village hall during half term. Entry is by donation with all proceeds to a charity in Thailand. Nolan's sister-in-law, Scheherazade, leading lady in this year's Wyeway pantomime, is director of the Thai charity. The chair of the village hall committee, Boris Dawes and his wife Doris will officially open the exhibition at a wine and cheese reception.

Tickets are £10 at the door.

Nosey Nolan: My Time

What do you know? I know who did what, when and to whom.

Ding Dong dell, the leading lady fell. Who wants her dead?

The stalker's out of bed. Oh no she's not!

Who believes in fairy tales? How long have you got? It's not a question I'd even considered this time last year.

Hickory Dickory Dock, the panto runs like a clock.

The clock struck eleven. Is toad prince in heaven?

Hickory Dickory Dock. Oh no he's not!

Ever kissed a toad… and got warts?

Where do you start? There was an end and a middle. I don't know what constitutes a beginning. Was it my return home after seven years in Australia? Or obsessions from cyberspace to lust? What came first – the players or the game?

Ring a ring o" Ring a ring o' roses. Our panto opens and closes.

Atishoo, atishoo, we all fell down.

A murder, a death, a stalker and a village pantomime – whatever it was, it certainly wasn't cricket!

Oh yes it is! Oh no it's not!

To me, the cricket pavilion in the village embodies the essence of English sport – order, tradition, competition and camaraderie. But it is the village hall that reveals the true measure of country life. These crumbling meeting places host a cross section of activity. From the parish council tug-o-war politics, to Women's Institute discussions on jam and justice, to mum and bub gaggles, to the village play, all are accommodated and tolerated.

In bygone days only male actors trod the boards. Men with swarthy stubbles and draped as young virgins delighted their audiences with moans, groans, winks and blinks. In post-modernity, village life has evolved. Now there are too many women for the amateur dramatic parts, never enough men and a scrum by both to bag the part they want. It's more an obstacle race than cricket.

Casting the annual pantomime in Wyeway is a major spectator event in itself. I'm not sure whether it is a penance or a prize but I'd been asked to write a seven hundred and fifty word feature about the opening performance for the local newspaper. I made headlines in the County Chronicle last month as the prodigal professor devoted to knowledge. Seven years in Australia and now I'm back on sabbatical. I've a book to complete with a six month deadline. Devotion's a funny word. It implies exclusivity, focus and passion… mostly directed towards a person or a cause. My sense of devotion is more mundane, an enthusiasm or a mild addiction. What else can I do but read and write? I'm unemployable in any other world. I wasn't called Nosey Nolan for nothing at school. Shy, gawky and hopeless at sport I struck lucky with research.

"Go hide at home," said my publisher. "You'll get the manuscript finished with no distractions."

Done and dusted, easy peasy, so they think. But home is a problematic word. Is home where you are born or where you are accepted? Wyeway or Toowoomba, Gloucestershire or Queensland, Britain or Australia? I am devoted to the idea of a home, always yearning for that faraway place but never quite settled. I return from one home to another with nowhere to hide.

My brief from the County Chronicle was to give a fair critique and be honest. If only I dared! Living in the village and being the brother of the script writer the truth poses a conundrum. As I wish to remain attached to my bollocks I will write only what needs to be read. And this year's pantomime has been something else.

A call to read *Snow White and the Seven Dwarves* rallied most able-bodied and feeble-minded residents of Wyeway. An evening of literary delight was promised with frozen sausage rolls and as much home brew as you could down in three hours. Frank, the volunteer in charge of lighting and all things technical, prides himself on skolling more pints per hour than Bill in sound effects. It got ugly by the end of the night. The drunks started to argue about the feuds from shows in yester years. Others vomited in the toilets and missed the pedestals despite the large poster above the washbasins.

Your HOME AWAY from HOME!
Take pride – this is your place.
Each and everyone is responsible for the care of Wyeway village hall.

Alcohol was banned one year by the Village Hall Committee (VHC).

A few seasons ago consensus transferred the script read-through to our local pub, the Turkey and Tree. That meant paying retail prices for beer. Herk, the publican, was delighted and sponsored an annual pantomime award for outstanding achievement. Quite how achievement was to be defined was left loose after heated committee debates. But no one could afford to get drunk at pub prices. This deviation was denounced as "too boring for words". It has been back to the village hall ever since, care notices and vomiting thespians notwithstanding. But the post-performance party on opening night is always held at the pub and Herk still offers his award.

I watched as Boris Dawes, the Chair of the VHC, greeted everyone at the door with a slobber on the cheek and a limp handshake. His wife, Doris, decked in her Sunday best, but minus her crocheted beret, stood beside him. With a forced smile she indicated the refreshments - entirely unnecessary as the refreshments have been in that place for twenty three years. Ever since a VHC decree was passed unanimously on the grounds that the expense of mop head replacements could be halved through judicious limitation of "messy areas."

"Clearly locals are more mindful of where they eat than where they urinate," I noted to my sister Belinda.

After first drinks or three were downed, the would-bes and the wannabes sat down on the hard-backed metal chairs ready to read the lines. The chairs were placed in a circle, cold to the touch but quick to warm up. Once heated their structural integrity was called into question as tiny squeaks erupted when any body bits moved. I'm told that on the first occasion when the chairs were used, Boris Dawes thought one of the VHC had the farts. Most of the committee chose to ignore the sounds at first. But after a while this became impossible. Doris took charge and tabled an emergency motion to suspend the meeting in the interests of health, safety and social decorum. No offender was found, despite Doris's thorough interrogation of all present. The result was a major agenda item at the following meeting. Lots of attempts have been made since that first meeting to rectify the problem. These range from lubrication with Vaseline, suggested by the womanising rogue who runs the local garage, to knitted joint rings, made by the Women's Institute group that use the hall on the first Tuesday of every month. Nothing has worked. The solution is elusive but Boris has it listed as a recurring item on the VHC agenda under Any Other Business.

There were four chairs placed at the top of the circle. These were reserved for the Writer, the Director, the Stage Manager and the VHC Chair. Boris and Doris donated the maroon, Draylon-covered club chairs to the VHC. The chairs are comfortable enough although in latter years the springs are not what they should be. Incumbents, especially portly ones, get stuck. According to Belinda, the Director had to be heaved out last year. Doris confided to me that the ensuring incident was a ploy by Scheherazade, the Leading Lady, to cement her bid for the role. She had placed her red-tipped talons into the Director's hands and decorously tugged. This resulted in her toppling from stiletto, knee length, purple, suede boots to land in his lap. Rumour has it that the Director winced, the VHC Chair scowled with jealousy and the rest of the cast fixated on the expanse of breast overflowing the décolleté of her dress. The Leading Lady claimed to have fainted.

"Friends, thespians and countrymen, lend me your ears," the VHC Chair welcomed. "In the spirit of the good bard I have come not to bury Caesar but to hand over to Belinda, the writer of this year's script. Her time to rise. My time to praise."

The throng clapped. Belinda looked nervously at the floor. I rolled my eyes and began to make notes. Frank burped. Rosalie, the stage manager, appeared to be assessing the shoes of the assembled as she compulsively folded and unfolded her hands in their fluffy purple mittens. Alice Sweet, who is a dead cert for the role of the Fifth Sheep, was almost beetroot tinged for the whole evening, such is her blushing adoration of Frank who failed to notice her pining fixation. Doris Dawes kept her eyes peeled on the Leading Lady who winked at Boris whenever the opportunity arose.

Belinda is a legend, the local girl made good. Our dad was a farm labourer, barely literate. Sporting ox proportioned pectorals and a dulcet tenor voice he dug ditches most of the day and sang half the night. Star of local music hall he was renowned for his pitch perfect and tear-inducing rendition of *You'll Never Walk Alone*. Belinda and I inherited none of his genes. She was petite and less than impressive as third backing singer with *It's in His Kiss* at the pub's karaoke nights. I never even passed the audition for the Sunday school choir in the nativity play.

What my sister lacked in musicality she compensated for with vocabulary. From top of her class in English throughout school she graduated from Oxford University with a first in English Literature and the gold medal for her essay on *Esotericism of the Second Generation of British Romantic Poets 1815-1837*. The hat trick was landing a job in the media.

"And you are?" smarmed Tom Prince, the celebrity actor, bolstered by fast sex and a diet of drugs.

"Belinda, TV researcher. Gosh, I can't believe you are talking to me."

"A snort or a fuck?" Tom replied.

She blushed. He was amused. They left the party together. Then it all went pear shaped. He scored a devoted, uncompetitive live-in, gourmet domestic. Belinda marvelled at her good fortune. She got pregnant and headed home to beyond the hills in order to roost in the family nest. Wyeway was thrilled to herald the homecoming queen and her soap opera king. Who quickly reverted to the pond frog he had always been. I call him the Toad Prince but not to his face. I love my sister and her children despite their spawning. Belinda says she approves of what seven years in God's Antipodean backwater have done for me. Such are sibling bonds.

Local sweepstakes reckon that Belinda's husband has bedded every female below thirty-five over the last six years. Latterly he seems keen to expand his horizon. On bonfire night he was caught *in flagrante* with the widow Jenkins - not a day under fifty-three. Her departed spouse, a devoted but dull accountant, bequeathed her a large inheritance and a healthy appetite for life. The result was surgically enhanced breasts, a face cranked in permanent smile and the predatory habits of a tom cat. Consensus is that Belinda's husband may be errant but he must be a skilled performer between the sheets.

When the village am-dram committee imploded for the fifth consecutive year after its attempts to collaboratively write a pantomime script, Belinda stepped in and offered to take on the job.

"A local girl with a gold medal for writing is not to be ignored," Boris had said.

Her offer was accepted and every female in the village looked forward to reading her work and meeting her husband, although not necessarily in that order.

This year's script, *Snow White,* followed last year's sell-out of *Jack and the Mechanical Beanstalk.* So successful was the engineering that the beanstalk refused to stop growing on the final performance, hit the ceiling, pushed through the trusses and damaged the roof tiles. In turn, this triggered the fire alarms, switched on the sprinkler system and automatically summoned all available fire engines from the neighbouring districts to the scene. It took a week to clear the sodden mess and a protracted meeting to appease the emergency services. But everyone agreed it was the pièce de résistance, the finale of a lifetime. I wish I had got to write that feature, warts and wobbles included.

Belinda prefaced the introduction to her script this year with a direct reminder.

"Snow White needs to make a substantial profit to offset last year's extravaganza. The cost of repairing the hall means that this year's offering must be produced on a much reduced budget."

Boris qualified this when he announced that the VHC had added a caveat: no moving parts to be used in the performance for any reason.

"If this is violated, in any way," chirped Doris, "all performances forever more will be cancelled."

The reading began. All did not go well. Before long, a major dispute erupted over representation of the seven dwarves.

"We don't have any dwarves in the village," said Boris.

"Improvisation will be a challenge," agreed Belinda.

Frank suggested using children. Alice clapped approval and added, "It would look cute." Others aye-ayed in support.

"The performances would be truly inclusive and cement community spirit."

"Bravo, small people are small people whatever the label."

Boris and Doris objected strongly.

"Everyone knows," they chimed, "that children today are undisciplined. We can't have them running amok in the village hall."

"Imagine the cost of the repairs," said Boris.

"We could lose our insurance cover," agreed Doris.

Frank looked askance when he saw the common support for this sentiment. The Director suggested that there might be problems having youngsters around. Something to do with family legislation and police record checks. Boris and Doris were vehement.

"Rubbish. There's nothing funny going on in our neck of the woods!"

Another suggestion was tossed into the debate.

"What about putting folks in wheelchairs? Make them look half size."

"Why would you want to that?"

"Where would we get seven wheelchairs?"

"Daft, couldn't get that many wheelchairs on the stage."

"This is not a play about disability rights."

Just when it looked as if the group might agree about the metaphorics of dwarfism on stage, Doris raised the temperature by introducing the thorny topic of which charity would benefit from the proceeds of the performances. No one wanted a donation to go to organisations linked to dwarves. Agreement on this settled the group but not for long. The debate presented lots of options for the target charity – local versus national versus international; children or adults; young people or the elderly; people or animals; buildings or causes. The list was endless. Finally, Belinda burst into tears. The hall went silent. Speculation was rife.

"Bet there's something untoward going down at home," murmured Boris to Doris.

"What can you expect with a sexpot husband?" Doris whispered back.

Belinda took a deep breath, put her sodden tissue back in her bag and spoke breathily.

"I would just like to say that we should all remember charity starts at home. If the rest of the meeting is going to be about shouting at each other I would prefer to withdraw my script and leave."

The group did not move. They knew Belinda would not withdraw her script. She has said this every year since she began writing them. The group recognized the signal.

"Enough is enough," said Boris.

"Time to finish," echoed Doris.

The following weeks were fraught with cast members trying to enlarge and re-write their parts, lobbing the Director for a more prominent role and aligning themselves into factions to ensure their opinion was delivered. It was to no avail. I know Belinda. She was very serious about withdrawing the rights to her script if a single word was altered without her authorisation. So the ritual went full circle. It was soon time to start rehearsals – a whole new round of simmering excitement and cold arguments commenced. It was three months until opening night. Tales and memories keep the village gossiping for months. I collected background fodder for my feature.

The meeting concluded with Frank staggering from the room to visit the toilets for a relief vomit. He won the drinking competition over Bill with a score of five pints per hour. Alice asked Belinda if she thought Frank had noticed her new shoes. Rosalie overhead the question. The look on her face suggested that Alice should pray that nobody noticed what she had on her feet.

"Are you going to check that Frank reads the notice in the toilets?" demanded Doris.

"'Nuff said, luv," muttered Boris.

"It's not you that has to clean up the mess."

"It won't be you either luv," replied Boris. "Leave it to the cleaners."

Belinda rang her husband. There was a short flurry of excitement. The women checked their attire and flicked their hair. HE was coming to collect her. His mobile was on but the toad didn't answer. The voice mail message clicked in. Belinda was nonchalant in a save-face kind of way. Others were most disappointed and showed it.

I offered to walk Belinda home. My sister's house was en route to mine. The nudge-nudging began. The Publicity Co-ordinator winked at the Front of House Manager. I knew bets were on for in whose bed Belinda's errant husband would be found. The Prompt wagered it would be the widow Jenkins, again. The Leading Lady didn't care because she had had a rendezvous with him last Wednesday. Alice was concerned about how Frank would stagger home and offered to drive him. Frank gagged. Alice blushed. They departed in separate directions.

Belinda and I walked in silence for some minutes before she asked, "So who will win the bet?"

"Who told you?"

"Walls and ears – same old, same old," she replied.

"Want to upset the game?

"Oh no, that wouldn't be cricket Mr Nolan."

"Oh yes it is," I replied.

"Oh no, brother dear, let's not start that."

"The old ones are the best," I said.

"Panto," quipped Belinda, "where did it all go wrong?"

"I'll bet on Shirley," I said with resignation. "She knows it's safe to entertain."

Belinda said nothing.

"A woman needs…" I mimicked, "Shirley will say that if it gets awkward."

She is good at justifying infidelity. What with her husband's impotence.

I should know. I'm her husband.

**Wyeway Amateur Dramatic Society
presents**

SNOW WHITE AND THE
SEVEN DWARVES

Directed by Harry Heil

**Written by Belinda Prince
(adapted from the Walt Disney story)**

Supported by Wyeway Village Hall Committee
Proceeds to Wyeway Retirement Settlement

Harry: Break a Leg

"Break a leg" assumes a whole new meaning when amateur thespians struggle through sleet to the village hall by five o'clock. It was the first rehearsal of the village pantomime, *Snow White*. Punctuality is the Director's second name. Wet coats, dripping hats and a parade of Wellington boots littered the Wyeway hall vestibule. Inside the motley masses were assembled, gently thawing, scripts in hand. The cast were eager to bond and begin.

"To be your leader I must be able to move the masses."

So spoke the Director, Harry Heil.

I jotted a note on a post-it and stuck it in my diary – *Google Führer quotations*. Word Perfect is not the Director's prerogative. Another note: *Is quote from advertising jingle? Medicine for diarrhoea?*

Dapper in British racing green cord trousers (straining over ample buttocks), a chunky, cable-knit, cream-flecked pullover with a green and orange paisley patterned, silk cravat (Jaeger label peeping), expensive and highly polished leather brogues (Church's sale item it is rumoured), I know Harry to be a man tolerated, venerated but not well liked. He commands an air of mystery with officious direction and pedantic warmth, juggling all three with consummate skill and total control.

Bets had been placed on which bastardised quotation from *Mein Kampf* the Director would sprout at the first rehearsal. Frank, from lighting, won. Alice Sweet, cast as the Fifth Sheep, greeted the news of the wager with a huge grin, a covert wink and loud applause. Frank blushed. Harry called for order.

"Only constant repetition of lines and movement will finally succeed in imprinting an idea on the memory of the audience," the Director said.

Another quotation. Would Hitler have been pleased that his words transferred so easily to an English village? Was it just director-speak for learn your lines or else? Or else what? I started to doodle. I captioned my efforts. I tried anagrams with the words: snow, white, seven dwarves. Anything to relieve the tedium of a pantomime rehearsal. I got as far as "No shit... never wave" before a horrible thought invaded – *remember Nolan you agreed to write a seven hundred and fifty word feature for the newspaper.*

Harry chose to bring his own cushion to put on the hall chair. He positioned the chair two metres from the side door and four metres and twenty two centimetres from the centre back of the hall precisely. The cast watched with trepidation and amusement whenever the Leading Lady went to talk to the Director. He stood. She manoeuvred so that his chair was always bumped, ever so slightly, off course. When she departed back to the stage, he re-positioned it. This would occur many times over the course of rehearsals according to her petulance and his patience. I noticed that Harry also lined up his pens to the right of his script, black pen closest, then red and finally green. A six centimetre pencil was placed mid-way along the top edge of the script. A green tumbler, brought from his home each rehearsal, was kept half full, ten centimetres from the edge of the table on which all of the above items were positioned. When the water level in the glass fell below the correct level, Harry topped it up from his personal bottle of still mineral water. I'm told by my sister Belinda that the kit, except for the chair and table which belong to the village hall, is packed and unpacked every rehearsal, every year, by Harry into his khaki bag on wheels for safe and efficient transportation. I speculated if a copy of *Mein Kampf* travelled too.

Opinions concerning the Director were as numerous as the cast itself. Some sympathised with his plight and aspirations.

"Ask a small man to do a big job," confided Doris Dawes.

"Such is the lone path of the man on a mission," offered Mr Nells, postman by day, rear half of the pantomime cow by night.

"He's brutal but fair," said Boris Dawes.

"I admire a man who is so well organised. It can't be easy," Doris agreed.

Others were more critical in their evaluations.

"Bloody Hitler!"

"Bullying is not a way to manage!"

"The Director would make a fascinating study in time and motion," I said to my sister, Belinda. "Perfect case study for a psychology student intent on analysing group dynamics."

"The man is the benevolent dictator of his stage kingdom," she replied.

"Exactly, dapper dress, military tidiness, obsessive attention to detailed movements on stage, a compulsive need to control all aspects of the performance. All powerful, well intentioned, he's got short man syndrome."

"Well that's one way of describing applause on opening night," Belinda laughed. "He's also called Harry Heil. What other reputation could he have?"

"Snow White, move stage right," demanded Harry. Snow White moved.

"Doc, Dopey and Grumpy, exit stage left," he shouted. Exit pseudo dwarves with the tap dancing trees.

"Prince Charming, enter before they exit."

Oh no, mis-timing resulted in a collision. The move was neither charming nor opportune. The Prince was annoyed. The rest of the cast laughed.

"Start again from page seventeen," Harry barked. "And where is the rest of the cow? All of it's supposed to be on stage for the whole scene."

"You mean me?" shouted Mr Nells from backstage. Harry sat and took three sips of water from his green tumbler.

Doris Dawes attended the first rehearsal. Traditionally she organises the donations from the cast to buy a present for the Director. In the interests of transparency she began to canvass opinion on what would be an appropriate gift. The first signs of rupture became apparent. Frank suggested a set of fine brushes and tubes of primary coloured acrylic paint.

"Why on earth would you give Harry that load of rubbish?" Belinda whispered to me.

"It's not a bad idea," I said. "He could make a model set of next year's pantomime to show you."

"I'm not writing another panto script."

"That's what you said last year and the year before that," I said.

The cast know that the present must be large enough to look good in the photo I had promised to take for the newspaper article; expensive enough to satisfy the Director's vanity; anonymous so that the cost and source remained a secret; and small enough for the Director to carry it home in his mobile kit bag.

According to Belinda, Harry's home has been a constant source of speculation over the years. No one has ever been invited to visit. There has never been a cast party or a pantomime committee meeting held at his place. Everyone knows where he lives. Nobody has ever entered.

"Lights, what's happened to the lights?" shouted the Director. The hall went dark. The pantomime cow bumped into Snow White.

"Oh Mr Nells," said the Leading Lady, "is that your horn I can feel?"

"Oh no it's not," the cast shouted, pleased by the diversion in the dark.

"Oooo yes it sooo is," said Snow White with a giggle.

"This is not funny," shouted Harry again.

"Oh yes it is," they all replied. Chaos threatened to rise to new levels.

Many moons ago, before I departed to Australia, I scored a part time job as a journalist with the *County Chronicle*. Eager to get a story, I called uninvited at Harry's home. I had hoped to persuade him to pose at his writing desk. I thought I could take a photograph to illustrate the director at work. It seemed such a good idea at the time. Belinda and I had speculated about his work space.

"His creative area will be a bunker with books, neatly arranged in alphabetical order," Belinda had suggested.

"Pride of position will be copies of Hitler's books in German with an English translation standing to the right of each volume," I added.

"Imagine reproductions – Third Reich, propaganda posters. Heil Harry!"

"Framed above a fireplace I bet."

I expected to discover a slate-tiled, stone hobbit house amongst ancient oak trees, meticulously maintained and spotlessly tidy. Armed with a camera and note book, I had headed off to door-step my quarry. Nosey Nolan, aspiring PhD candidate, investigative news reporter, fait accompli.

The sober reality half-hid down a track, off a strip road, up a hill, and nearly three kilometres from the nearest bitumen, county maintained, B-road.

Hitler in Hicksville, I recorded in my notebook. The Director resided in a modern bungalow, ugly as. With pebble-dashed walls in need of a paint job, the house sported plastic windows, the double-glazed, monstrosities of mass advertising and poor taste. The garden was mostly concrete, of the crazy-paved variety, with plastic pots of wilting flowers and thirsty evergreens turning brown or sporting mildew from winters past.

How does a man with a stage mission flourish amongst such a torpid set?

I approached the house. I knocked on a poo-coloured door. A man's voice, answered from inside.

Shit and derision were my first thoughts. Harry, the Director, was not a solitary bachelor with an exotic lair to seduce and dally with the ladies. Was he gay?

"Don't answer the door. We're not at home," I heard the Director's voice shout in the background.

Too late, a munchkin, wrinkled with age and genetic haphazardry, short and morbidly obese, had opened the door wide, curious and eager to meet a new face. In his hand he held a gaudy, half-painted garden gnome. Behind him I saw that there were tens, maybe hundreds of these gnomes. Gnomes sitting on tables, lying on chairs, balancing on stools, littering the floor – a convention of reject might-have-beens waiting to escape.

"You want me bruvver?" smiled the munchkin.

I was transfixed by the utter chaos inside the house. There could be no special area in which Harry contemplated and blocked his annual pantomime script. Director and house proud did not rhyme.

Where does a man find space to imagine amidst such squalor?

I shuddered. Harry walked to the door, resignation and despair etched on his face. Tears pricked his eyes as he saw me, the eager, new journalist, official gossip monger for the village. Empathy? Sympathy? Angry?

How does a man morph into a mouse?

"Et tu, Brute?" the Director quoted at me. He slammed the door shut. A pained wail from the mutant brother inside pierced the isolation. No more visitors that day. I walked away. Like Caesar, the Director waited for his fall.

So the Director was a pantomime Führer in name only.

88

A small man, pummelled by circumstances to fulfil a silent role. Who could be vicious about a mini-man with a giant's responsibilities? Who wants to be a full time carer for an aged brother with Down's syndrome?

I have never mentioned my visit to anyone, not even Belinda. Like Hitler's remains, speculation about the Director's private life continued to buzz beyond cold evidence. Even wannabe journalists and academics, impoverished by investigative leads, desperate for results and committed to truth at all costs, can recognise sacred boundaries. Some things are best left alone. The Director's secret will always be safe with me.

But this year a silent salute has marked my return to Wyeway. After each rehearsal that I have attended, a gift appears at my back door. Yet another painted gnome had found its special home.

GONE WITH THE WIND
...live the dream ... live the dream ... live the dream...

Scarlett centre stage in white

	Re: Forthcoming stage show By sweet and sexy Snow White >>> 1830 Just to let ya all know, Scarlett needs a diversion to warm up these cold winter nights. While Rhett is away, I plan to play. Ever heard the one about a gal called Snow White?
	Re: Forthcoming stage show By Rhett Butler 189 >>> 1845 My dear, I may not be a gentleman but Snow White is no lady. Cavorting with seven dwarves in the woods???
	Re: Forthcoming stage show By Rhett Butler 532 >>> 1910 Honey child I is coming to see ya lily white body on da stage. Then I is gonna show you ma gun, cocked for action, after dem curtains have closed. Hang on tight, dis cowboy is ready for action my little chickadee!
	Re: Forthcoming stage show By Nosey academic >>> 1930 I'm an anthropologist doing research into

community activities which promote positive social networking. Let me know if you would like to participate in a questionnaire.

Re: Forthcoming stage show
By sweet and sexy Snow White >>> 1948

OMG – what can this leading lady say? Boys, I just adore your adoration. But sweet little ol' me and all things academic with those big words are not going to work.

Re: Forthcoming stage show
By Rhett Butler 532 >>> 2034

Honey child who needs words? Your man in the saddle is after action.

Re: Forthcoming stage show
By sweet and sexy Snow White >>> 2040

Fiddledee dee cowboy Rhett, you take my breath away!

Re: Forthcoming stage show
By Rhett Butler 532 >>> 2043

My little chickadee keep a breathing. I is coming to find you, no mountain high enough to keep me from riding to your side. And honey child, just remember, a man in your hand is worth more than 7 short arses anywhere.

	Re: Forthcoming stage show By sweet and sexy Snow White >>> 2046 What a naughty boy you are Cowboy Butler! You make me blush with excitement.
	Re: Forthcoming stage show By Rhett Butler 532 >>> 2310 Honey child I is looking forward to seeing you blush, all over.

Alice: How Men See Me

It was tense back stage the night of the dress rehearsal.

"Fiddledee dee, great balls of fire," said Alice Sweet with a note of panic. She fidgeted with the tail of her Fifth Sheep costume. It defied gravity.

"Don't call me sugar," she instructed in a ludicrous attempt at a deep-south American drawl.

I couldn't see that the order was addressed to a person.

"I didn't call you anything," I said, stepping out of the shadows back stage.

Alice blushed, "Oh Professor Nolan, I didn't see you there."

"Are you practising your lines?" I asked.

Alice replied that her part was twenty lines in total with one line repeated. She got to say, "Oh no it's not a dwarf singing hi ho" once in act one, twice in act two. She confided that the remaining seventeen lines revealed the same depth of characterisation and scope for delivery. Quite why her character needed to speak with an American accent was not clear. I didn't think it was a good time to ask.

"I'm sure your part is essential to the success of this show," I consoled.

"It's pantomime," she said to me, "in a village with a population of one hundred adults and pumpkin-faced kids in nappies!"

"Can't really comment," I explained. "The script and me, we're related."

Alice nodded in sympathy.

The Fifth Sheep had three more lines than the sixth sheep and three less than the fourth. It is not for nothing that my sister Belinda, the script writer, enjoys a reputation for numeracy, fairness and accuracy. The tenth sheep had a mere five lines and was struggling with those. Not the words themselves, just the order of delivery. But the cast and village understand. How wonderful that Myrtle, she of tenth sheep fame, can still tread the boards with Alzheimer's.

However, at this rehearsal, it was obvious that the Fifth Sheep was not a happy mutton chop. I understood that she has complained for the last three years, since she progressed from eighth sheep, that her costume was not right.

"What do you think it does for your self-confidence?" she whimpered to me and anyone who would listen. Nobody did listen. The cast were too busy preening in their own costumes, lovingly stitched from abandoned curtains and old pillow cases, by Mrs Reece and her fleet of biddies. The loyal seamstresses were from the retirement village. They chomped on their false teeth as they sewed a last minute, distressed hem or two.

I couldn't help but sympathise with the Fifth Sheep. Her costume was a sack made from synthetic, fire retardant stuffing. It might have worked wonders for health and safety in a sofa but it did little for a thirty something, avocado shaped, virgin-in-hope.

"How men see me," she groaned. Alice proceeded to tell me the history of the garment. It was originally made to fit a morbidly obese eleven year old in the school's nativity play. There's plenty of width which the Fifth Sheep tried to pleat. Those tucks merely emphasised her ample waist. The real structural challenge lay in the length. The original model was ten centimetres shorter. The Fifth Sheep struggled with the scratchy material. The ever rising crutch of the costume threatened the circulation to her private parts and did not titillate by what it revealed.

"God please let me get promoted to third sheep next year," she said to me. At my blank look she told me that particular costume had been constructed for the tallest boy in the primary school.

"Better still persuade Belinda to make me second tree. Then I get to swank on stage in a silky green satin sheath."

"I'm afraid it's the Director who makes all those decisions," I said. Could it be that the real objective of the Fifth Sheep was to wake up Frank, the short-sighted fellow on the lighting rig, and show him what he might enjoy?

Alice Sweet was not without virtue and plaudits. According to Belinda, Alice got a lot of mentions in the local press during the late summer. Marrows apparently, Alice grows marrows. They won local fetes. Jealous detractors whispered that their size could not be natural. Last year there had been a burglary. The door to her garden shed had been forced. Alice told the police that nothing appeared to have been stolen. Rumour had it that the unwelcome visitor was a neighbour sent to spy. The crucial question was: had steroids been used to enhance marrow growth? Bets were placed on who did what and when. Doris Dawes added to the gossip with her theory that the perpetrator was the Stage Manager, Rosalie Curtis as she was the recognised expert on all things scientific in the village. With the marrows that didn't win ribbons the Fifth Sheep made jam for the pantomime cast.

"No surprises this year?" Doris enquired. "I thought you might have followed my advice and added some ginger."

Alice's life might have seemed drab to most of the village. However, they've underestimated her ability to find joy and fulfilment. She has a secret pleasure. By sheer chance I discovered that the Fifth Sheep was a member of an Internet group dedicated to the virtual re-enactment of *Gone with the Wind*. It might have been her secret in the village. But to the on-line membership she was a goddess, the living embodiment of everything Scarlett O'Hara was and ever could be. She was word perfect with the script. Her southern American drawl was enticingly authentic. Scarlett's wardrobe moulded perfectly to her avatar body. Numerous Rhett Butlers duelled for her favour. In cyberspace they saw only her perfection.

I wouldn't have recognised her other self. I was amused to see what the Fifth Sheep had added about her theatrical enterprises to the site's daily blog. Some things were not to be shared in either direction, it seemed. But I was curious why the woman in the unflattering romper suit was so tense, fidgety and speaking to thin air in an American accent at this dress rehearsal. She knew her lines and cues well.

Most of the cast avoided her along with the rest of the sheep. Their costumes stank from years of sweating under the lights. The fabric doesn't breathe. It can't be washed. There was no budget for dry cleaning. No one was permitted to take their costume home from the village hall, ever, for any reason. Orders came from the Director and Stage Manager about this. To disobey might mean demotion or even exclusion from next year's play. Sheep act as sheep are. Conformity gave strength in numbers.

"What's wrong?" I asked as I took her aside. "You'll be fine. And the costume is okay. Especially when all the sheep are on stage. Looks kind of cute actually."

"You don't understand," she said and burst into tears.

"Try me."

"I've told a lie," she blubbered.

"We all tell lies," I cajoled. "Didn't Scarlett tell a few to make life work?"

"You know?" she gasped.

"Your secret's safe with me."

"How did you find out?"

"First principle of journalism, never reveal your

sources. Nobody here knows about your Scarlett or follows the blog. I promise I won't say anything."

"Yes but Rhett might!"

"Sorry, you've lost me," I said and handed her a tissue. Sheep make-up was running down her cheeks.

"Rhett Butler, number 532, from Reading is coming. He's emailed me. He says nothing can deter him from attending my play. He's pledged to travel to wherever I'm performing."

"Well that's wonderful isn't it? He'll get to see you can play lots of different roles. Versatile can be very sexy."

"Somehow he thinks I'm the leading lady," she sobbed.

"Well you can clear that up when you meet. Honestly that costume is passable. It certainly shows off your legs. And beige is a good colour on stage under the lights."

"He thinks it's a professional production."

"He'll work out that it's not. But don't worry. You're good. Really good. I'm sure a fifth sheep on the London stage wouldn't do the role any better than you."

"The Seduction of Snow White by the Dalek Dwarfs," she wailed.

"What?"

"I might have said that the name of the show was…"

"He's in for a bit of a surprise then. It's a bit more wholesome than he is probably expecting."

"A snuff script on stage," she cried. "That's what he circulated to the group."

I couldn't think of an honest reply.

"What else did he email you to say?"

"Show me your apples and I'll show you my banana."

The Fifth Sheep disappeared to hide backstage. Her unmasking was imminent. There could be a no more dramatic denouement. I could see that to tell the truth would ruin her life on this patch of earth in addition to the potential out there in a virtual world. I found her behind the props table in a yoga position. She was slow breathing as if to inhale the original pain of Vivien Leigh and Clark Cable. She exhaled when she saw me and shouted one of the film's immortal lines: *With enough courage you can do without a reputation.*"

I didn't remember who said it but...

I felt for Alice. Her dilemma as the Fifth Sheep was manifold. There would be no credits to roll if she was named and shamed to her band of Margaret Mitchell groupies. No more would she be Scarlett in cyberspace. No more would she be adored by Rhett Butlers around the world. Nobody would give a damn. Not even Frank from lighting!

A Forest Fairytale

There were smiles all round when the leading lady of Wyeway saw her wish come true. £2000 was presented to Scheherazade James, who will play Snow White in the forthcoming pantomime. "It's a fairytale ending which will help disadvantaged women in a very poor community," she said collecting the cheque from Boris and Doris Dawes of the Wyeway Village Hall Committee.

The money was raised from the September exhibition of photographs by Professor Godfrey Nolan. Mounted in the village hall, the images documented his seven year residency in Toowoomba, Australia.

Proceeds from the exhibition will contribute to the work of Street Workers, for whom Scheherazade is UK director. The charity offers medical care and re-training to women in Thailand who are forced into prostitution by poverty.

Nearly 600 women who work the street bars in the popular tourist area of Patpong in Bangkok have taken advantage of the charity's resources and programmes over the last three years. Many of these women are keen to acquire secretarial, business and administration skills so that they can gain employment in the hotel and hospitality sectors.

Scheherazade: **Gloom, Doom or Bloom**

Another night, another rehearsal, another story. The Leading Lady in the pantomime has the unlikely name of Scheherazade. Like her namesake, she's exotic and flamboyant, petite, slim-hipped, long-legged with ebony hair pendulous and lustrous. If not for the disproportionately large breasts I might have described her as a nymph. She kept the Director awake, the cast motivated and the backstage crew captivated. People were seduced by her beauty and aroused in her presence. The pantomime was really just another branch of her fan club. Everyone was eager to please, male and female, young and old. Scheherazade ought to know. She'd bedded most of them! Together with all and sundry around the valley and then beyond when the occasion presented. Her appetite is legendary – hetero, homo and bi – take your pick. As far as I know it's all been orthodox activity, no deviant parley with goats or rubber inflatables and the like.

Hercules (*poor bastard with that name*) or Herk the Turk as the village affectionately calls the publican, reckoned she is a nymphomaniac.

"Man, what a night!" he boasted.

But the village have long memories and smirked at his remark.

"Yeah – one night only," muttered Frank.

"Unforgettable, a night to remember. I deserved an Oscar," added Herk.

"So how come she never returned for a repeat performance?"

"You reckon those pups are natural?" salivates Boris Dawes.

There has been much speculation about her breasts. I've seen the photograph of Scheherazade's mother, a woman with Chinese ancestry a generation back.

"For sure her mother had feline eyes and dainty feet," said Herk.

"Yeah but did she have big tits?"

It's not only the village cats that have claws.

The Leading Lady displays eclectic taste in our monthly, clandestine meetings following my return from Australia.

"Feed the stomach, sustain the soul," she insisted.

Scheherazade and I have taken it in turns to choose a place to eat. Our budget is strict, ten pounds to include a drink. In six months I have never second guessed what she will select. Egg fried rice with toffee apples, on the same plate, in the House of Hong Kong. Ice cream pizza in Angelo's Trattoria. Lentil burger and apricot jam with rocket leaves in the Railway Café. Scheherazade swears it isn't a game. She claims to really love her selections.

"Outside the box, savour the taste," she said.

"Shit and derision, you're not going to order cardboard and custard are you?"

"Could be wicked," she suggested. "Good food and sex are all about new combinations."

Last month it was Thai cuisine. I'm a philistine. I went for green curry with sticky Jasmine rice. Scheherazade devoured chips dipped in Tom Yum soup.

"Reality chefs on television wouldn't stand a chance," I reckoned.

Neither would Shirley Nolan, my wife, understand the arrangement. A man's needs do not always match the stereotype. When Scheherazade and I had shared our counter intuitive, semi-orgasmic fodder we got down to the basic stuff of our interludes. We debated the debauched.

"Lady Chatterley lusted after love, not sex," Scheherazade argued.

"You reckon she was clued up enough to know the difference?" I asked.

The Leading Lady laughed. I relaxed.

"What about Heathcliff?"

"Anemometer-phobic, sleep-deprived, obsessive-compulsive. Should have been sectioned and admitted to a clinic in the central business district," she replied.

"See you're still a core romantic then."

Over six months we've read 30 classics novels from the top 100 list of all-time, romantic books. We agreed that *Gone with the Wind* was the big winner whatever the critics and book sale figures suggested. The academic in me tried to impress her with the breadth and depth of my Internet research about our idol.

"Just read the book and drink the words, eat the meaning. Screw what everyone else thinks. Live in the literature," she commanded. "What can Internet research offer?"

"If only you knew," I whispered. "Gloom, doom and bloom don't begin to describe it."

"You're not doing porn in cyberspace are you?" she asked.

"If that worked I wouldn't be here at the hospital, would I?"

"I think maybe you're lucky."

"How do you work that out?" I asked.

"Your wife's a slag."

"Thanks. Want to add any more compliments about your sister while you're in full voice?"

"Shirley must really love you."

"You arrived at that conclusion, how?"

"Shagging is shagging. And she's a serial shagger. So you know my sister's not with you for the rumpty pumpty stuff. You're not loaded. So that proves she's not a gold digger. You're not a famous TV personality like Belinda's bloke. Shirley must really be into your writing and your brain. Bit like the guy with the big nose."

"Pinocchio?"

"No duh," she said in mock despair. "Cyrano, Cyrano de Bergerac. I misquote: no trousers and all mouth."

"Not bad," I said, "but I've got a better one. And it's Thai."

"Go on then."

"Coconut shells float, stones sink."

"Nice image. Gold star for linking food and thought. How long did it take you to source it?"

"Not long," I admitted. "I'm doing some research on Thai mail order brides."

"You're changing the topic," she said.

"Yeah," I said, "let's leave Shirley to Mills and Boon."

"So how many others have you got?" she asked.

Scheherazade collects wise words. She and I joust with pithy adages compiled from our travels and research. It has become a friendly match with rival lists. Neither of us can claim to win. Neither of us is clearly defeated. What might be is always relevant to an academic. I have the longer list, Scheherazade the broader source. Our theme for that particular lunch echoes the menu – sayings from the Far East.

"Enter as a whirlwind, depart as an ant," I offered.

"Boat capsizes, the shark eats," she countered.

"That's really romantic!"

"Think I should use it on my stalker?" she asked.

With the wisdom of hindsight I wonder about that question. What should I have answered? If I had my time again...

"Wasted! It's bound to be someone in the panto," was what I said. "Sort of a theatrical wet dream. Maybe one of those blokes in lighting? Frank what's his name?"

"No," she said," Frank's too shy. And the Fifth Sheep'd poison me."

I laughed at the thought. "If the girl's too shy to flirt with Frank, I think you're safe on stage and off."

"You know she grows castor beans in her allotment. They're poisonous."

"Can be. Or they can keep you regular," I joked.

"You know how to say good words at bad times."

"Thanks, I think."

"The gifts are getting more creepy" she admitted.

"You got another one?"

"Two this week, one last."

"What were they this time? More cuddly toys?" I asked.

"As if! Try bits of cat. A real cat. One tail, two ears and four paws, dried blood sticky."

"Shit and derision, that's nasty. Report it. Someone's trying to scare you."

"Do you think they've found out?"

"You told anyone?"

"No, only you."

"What about the doctor? Didn't he want to know?"

"They don't ask. Abortions are bog standard. If you sign the forms they don't go there."

"I didn't mean the medic at this hospital clinic."

"I get all my treatment here now. Pernicious Anaemia, womb scraping, contraception. One stop shopping."

"You know he could get struck off. It's illegal and unethical to get involved with a patient."

"Bit inevitable. What was work? What was pleasure? Same thing?"

"Wasn't it my sister who said charity begins at home?"

"Bollocks! Belinda writes panto scripts."

"No regrets?"

Scheherazade stared through me and said quietly, "Want a thing long enough and then you don't."

"How do you know he wouldn't have seen it as an "our" baby. You, him and the bump. He wasn't exactly a wham bam."

"If he didn't commit to me after three years he was never going to commit," she said.

"A wife is a good reason not to do a public declaration. Forever into the sunset, dear heart and all that."

"His Thai wife got what she wanted – a UK visa."

"Maybe he wanted more?"

"Maybe he should have said more then."

We retreated to drinking the remains of our jasmine tea. Scheherazade tilted the petite china bowl and swirled the tepid liquid. I watched. The silence nurtured our intimacy.

"Is doctor dad still doing volunteer work with your charity?" I asked.

"Yes."

"So how is that working out?"

"Easy – delegated to one of my staff.

"You're not worried?"

"She's a lesbian. Not the lipstick variety."

Charity – it's hard work. Scheherazade manages a non-governmental organisation. It provides training in alternative employment for prostitutes in Patpong, Bangkok.

"How's the rise and fall of the crown jewels?" she asked.

"Let sleeping dogs lie," I retorted. The consultants can find no physical reason for my erectile dysfunction. My psychological evaluation stated "without obvious psycho-sexual traumas or delusions."

"We're not playing word games any longer."

Scheherazade is unsympathetic. She considers sex to be

overrated. She might be right. After all she's got lots of experience as a sex junkie rescuing sex slaves. I see life differently. Doesn't every impotent middle aged man?

"You're a bit of a waste of tax payers' money then?" Scheherazade smiled.

Does a platonic mistress count as benefit or a placebo?

"Aren't there many ways to skin a cat?" I replied.

"You are beyond redemption," she said.

"I hope so. It'll be lonely in hell without you."

We spent another five minutes discussing her course of Vitamin B jabs and continuing medication for Pernicious Anaemia.

"No new advice?" I asked.

"They tell me I shouldn't get pregnant for a year or three."

"That'll give you time to find an unmarried father for twins."

"Do I look like the sort of girl you'd take home to mum?"

"With your acting talent you could be anyone to any audience. The gossips are dying for another performance of your fainting fatale."

"That was genuine. I knew I had the lead role. I mean who else is there to be the drama diva?"

"Doris Dawes could give you a run for the role," I replied. "She does dramatic sighs better than anyone in the village."

We both chuckled at the preposterous image of erstwhile, crimplene-pleated Doris in purple suede boots swooning over the Director.

"I just fainted. It's what happens with this wretched condition."

"Another secret story. Another misunderstanding," I said.

"How could Snow White be less than perfect? My fans demand it of me."

"Perfection is like beauty. Eye of the beholder and all that?"

"You think I'm beautiful?" she asked.

"Nah, too subtle for me. I like my women blonde and bulimic. Preferably not too bright. Even better if they own a bald cat. Makes me look stunning."

"You are so not cool," she commented.

"I'm flattered," I said. "You could pass as an Aussie you know."

"In what way?"

"Your directness. You say it as you see it."

Seven years in Toowoomba and I acquired a new vocabulary and an alternative perspective. A pioneering town at the top of the Great Dividing Range, it was noted for its flower festival. The blossoms might be diverse, the people were not. Words like subtle and gentle simply didn't exist. Try in your face, between your eyes, point blank meaning, no innuendo, precise as. When I arrived, pasty-legged and cricket savvy, the rawness of the culture and language made me choke with incredulity. How could people be that blunt? By the time I left, I admired the honesty and integrity that accompanied the shock of delivery. It seemed that if an Aussie thought you were worth communicating with, then he gave it straight. When I suggested that bodyline bowling did disturb the great Donald Bradman I was derided as a 'Pommie bastard' and made to swim naked in a public pool in Toowoomba. Then I had my head flushed in a pub urinal before the town's cricket veterans bought me eleven rounds of beer and carried me home.

"Shirley must've found it easy then," Scheherazade smiled.

"Shirley and easy aren't words I'd put together."

"You sound like a father."

Ouch, a googly. I ranked Joe James as a dibbly dobbly in the father stakes. He sired two children and abandoned both their mothers. My wife Shirley was five when he finished his bacon and eggs and walked her to school for a nine o'clock start. By eleven he was enjoying pikelets, strawberry jam and a new flat with the nubile, mixed race teenager who had come to work in his office as part of her college course. It was work experience beyond the curriculum objectives. Two years later Scheherazade appeared. When the baby with the exotic name turned four, Joe James exited. His role as doting father was finished.

"Sticks and stones and what do they say about bones?" asked my sister-in-law. I ignored Scheherazade's attempt at an apology. Too difficult to go there.

"Female bones are very useful to forensic anthropologists," I replied, "mitochondrial DNA and all that. Mother's are the real worth. We can trace a family genealogy through women's bones. Men are redundant."

"Thank you Professor Nolan."

The alarm on my watch shrilled. Our monthly rendezvous was over. Time to go, sour minutes. She headed to her car, prancing in high-heeled, sunshine-coloured, strappy sandals. I shuffled to mine, an undone shoelace trailing like an anchor. We both had to head back to our sunset realities in the valley. Worlds apart, where we were not safe from local eyes. Scheherazade had her band of Rhett Butlers and charming princes. I had Shirley Nolan. A story with a happy ending? About as happy as dead cats in a hall of dwarves!

Order of International Meritus

awarded to

Dr Rosalie Curtis

in recognition of her outstanding
contribution to and pursuit of excellence
in the field of kinetic physics

Rosalie: Okay Not

A caricature of Rosalie Curtis, the pantomime's Stage Manager, is pinned to the notice board in my study. Sketched by Frank who does the lighting and all things technical, it depicts her as a dingo in sheep's clothing with stiletto hooves. But that pint-sized, Australian-born package of frilly collars, purple fluffy jumpers and crimped tawny hair is a fame-brain, now retired.

The cast call Rosalie "SS" to her face. She takes it as a compliment on the assumption that it is an abbreviation of her role in the production. I thought the initials underpinned her allegiance to Harry Heil and the Director's alter ego. The cast christened her SS, short for Shit on Stilts, my sister, Belinda, told me.

"Okay," I heard SS say in response to the Director's call for plastic apples that the pantomime cow could juggle. Quite how she would marry that request with the Village Hall Committee directive against any moving objects on stage was a tough challenge.

"Okay not," she snapped at Frank when he demanded that she supply a thirty metre extension cord. He needed the length to provide a reading light for the Prompt.

Belinda's hypothesis is that the Stage Manager tries to apply scientific theory to man management. It seems to me that understanding energy and controlling reactions was no more successful at rehearsals than it was in academia.

"So what is your big problem about lights?" Frank asked.

"Why do quantum dots start blinking in a pattern suggesting fractal kinetics after absorbing photons of light?" the Stage Manager retorted.

"Are you feeling alright?" Frank asked her.

"Okay, yes," Rosalie said. "There is not a short answer

to my research on lights. It's a complex field."

"Fuck – I don't want to read anything. Just yes or a no – can you get me an extension lead?"

"It is not okay to deploy coarse language back stage," she admonished, clip-clopping away in patent, mauve, ankle boots, before turning back to command, "Health and safety, get the prompt to wear a battery operated, head lamp."

"SS dingo's gone doolally again," Frank reported to his gang of aspiring technicians.

"I saw a really interesting documentary on dingoes," said Alice Sweet, the actress playing the Fifth Sheep.

I watched Frank's surprise at this outburst from the plump figure, suited in a fake astrakhan romper, lurking behind his equipment bin.

"Did you know that dingoes don't bark?" the Fifth Sheep continued.

"What?" said Frank.

"And dingoes have joints in their legs that rotate. They can turn door knobs."

"Sorry?" asked Frank.

"I'm into stuff on the Internet," explained the Fifth Sheep.

"Maybe she's into dogging," said a technician smirking at Frank.

"Well I'm not really into dogs. I was just researching dogs on American plantations during the civil war," she replied with honest innocence, "and I found out all this stuff about wild dogs."

"Wild dogging," sniggered another stage hand. "Tell us more, sweetie."

Alice glanced at Frank and blushed. "Dingoes can turn their head one hundred and eighty degrees in both directions. They've got ears that are permanently erect," she said.

"Wow, so now we know. Old SS herself is always up for it!"

"She's got eyes in the back of her head."

"She can open doors with a weak wrist."

"She likes knobs."

"Owww," howled one technician.

"Woof, woof," barked another.

"I really don't get you lot," Alice said.

"Leave her alone," commanded Frank.

The Fifth Sheep looked to Frank with gratitude. Frank blushed. The technicians grinned. Alice retreated. The clatter of the Stage Manager's heels alerted the technicians that SS was about to re-appear. No one was keen to stray into the orbit of SS any more than needed be. Or prepared to explain the term dogging to Alice or SS.

"Out of here," ordered Frank.

The group scurried to the safety of the gallery area where a Mecca of cables, tools and equipment offered respite and respect. The only person who fared worse with the Stage Manager's tongue lash was the Fifth Sheep. I couldn't understand why Alice was the object of SS's scoffing. Belinda said it could be linked to SS's fixation on shoes.

"The Fifth Sheep wears Wellingtons when it's wet; Mary Jane's for best; Trainers for winter wear; Crocs in summer and fake leopard skin slippers for indoors," explained Belinda.

Women and shoes were under my radar. I took it that Alice opted for comfort and a chiropody-free life.

"Is that manure?" SS enquired when she noticed something suspicious underfoot.

"Gosh, sorry," replied Alice, "I was gardening in these shoes."

"Health and safety okay! I understand you use chemical substances to fertilise?"

113

"My marrows win prizes because I only use organic matter," said Alice with pride. "It's a scientific fact that big and beautiful is linked to a respect of Mother Nature."

"It is not okay to pollute the stage with excrement, whatever its molecular structure," retorted Rosalie.

The cast gossip was that SS reserved her admiration and desire for the Leading Lady's collection of shoes. The piece de resistance was Scheherazade's stiletto-heeled, knee-length, purple suede boots when she had fainted into the lap of the Director at the script read-through. SS had had a glazed look when she removed the boots, ostensibly to help with recovery.

"SS looked positively orgasmic stroking that purple hide," Belinda confided.

Spot on!

"You know she classifies footwear. Those boots would be filed as examples of wearable art, category AAA: GK," said Belinda.

"You've lost me."

"SS tried to explain to me once – scholar to scholar kind of. The triple A designates crème of the elite. GK indicates that Galileo's laws of Kinetics…"

"What?"

"Something to do with energy from motion. It links distance with time I think. The point is that this theory stuff moulds her perception of the shoes," explained my sister.

"Well I think it's remarkable just how fast our Leading Lady can walk down country lanes in her heels."

"It's kind of sweet really. SS has ranked nearly everyone's shoes."

"That is too sad. How do I rate with three year old trainers?"

"Off the scale, brother dear. SS told me that she rates

most of the Leading Lady's foot wear under double A, although the bulk falls into a lower order of GN."

Sounds like bra sizes, I thought.

"GN denotes gravitation. Apparently it's based on Newton's three laws of motion. SS believes there is a clear link between the height of shoe heels and gravity," said Belinda.

"Why would you spend time analysing the heels on shoes?"

"We all have our foibles. Don't be so harsh," Belinda said. "SS doesn't discuss her deductions with me."

Well that's a relief.

"I guess she is emphatic enough to appreciate that not many of us could grapple with the underlying theory."

You're not wrong.

"However, I've noticed SS has a photographic memory. She can recognise a pair of Dior's from Dolce and Gabbana's at twenty paces," admitted Belinda.

That'll help climate change.

I thought back to the years before I went to Australia when I was reading for my doctorate. Newly married, broke but erstwhile, I was grateful for the part time work on the *County Chronicle*. The newspaper assigned me to do an interview with Rosalie Curtis. She had won an Order of International Meritus for her contributions to scientific understanding. The editor figured that I could talk to her, an academic kind of thing.

"Rosalie is a professor no less," I confided in fear to my sister Belinda. "Her publishing record in chemical physics is something else."

"So is her library of heels. Could rival Manolo Blahnik," Belinda replied in admiration.

Who?

"What do you reckon – Asperger's?"

"Maybe," said Belinda. "You never know with scientists. Theory turns them on, not people."

So I did my homework, compiled a list of her publications in my notes and rehearsed the pronunciations of scientific terms to an impressive level of fluency. "Congratulations Professor Curtis," I began, "you must be very pleased."

"Alcohol and intellect are not a chemical equation of commercial value, okay?" she answered.

I realised my carefully plotted approach would not work.

No idea what she was talking about.

"Sorry?"

"The Fair Dinkum," she replied.

"Haven't tried one," I said, feeling awkward. "It's Hurk's idea. He wanted the Turkey and Tree to honour your Queen's Birthday award."

"Naming a cocktail at a pub?"

"Australian – Herk called it a Fair Dinkum after you. He's trying hard to please."

"Okay, but not original."

"It's purple. Purple is a noble colour," I said, surveying her sitting room. I was unsettled sitting amongst such intense shades. The walls were mauve, the curtains were purple gingham with frilled pelmets, and the carpet was aubergine. I still shudder when I recall the ambience.

Like being buried alive in stale puke.

"Not okay with purple?" Rosalie asked.

"You clearly like living with it."

"What do you know about purple?" she interrogated.

I wanted to say that it was the colour of batty old ladies but I guessed that wouldn't get me an extended interview.

"Okay so dotty dames and Phoenician princes have made it famous," she said.

Alliteration!

116

I panicked.

"Do you know anything about the science of purple?" she continued.

I shook my head.

"Electromagnetic spectrum? Didn't they teach you that at school?"

"They tried," I said. "I did better in biology."

"Okay – a summary of purple. The electromagnetic spectrum describes energy – from cosmic rays to radio waves. Energy travels in waves. The distance between successive waves is called a wavelength. The number of times a wave moves between two points in a second is called frequency. The general rule is simple: the longer the wavelength, the lower the frequency. Purples have the shortest wavelengths, the highest frequencies and the most energy. In geometry the colour purple is represented by the dodecahedron."

Should I mention I also failed maths?

"It's my sister who's really the scholar," I said. "I've got a wife who's good with graphics and design."

"Your wife has excellent shoes. Purple Prada's. Your sister does not," Rosalie replied. "The dodecahedron is the most complex of the Sacred Geometry shapes. Ancient Greeks... Platonic Solids... illuminating. Study the classics?"

I shook my head and began to sweat.

How could I take notes? I didn't understand the questions.

"Okay, a simple explanation. Plato was a Greek philosopher. He believed that there were five basic shapes and their proportional relationships affect our perception. So for solid objects the lengths of the sides are all equal, and all interior angles are equal."

"You mean like triangles and stuff?" I asked.

117

"Okay, yes. Triangles traditionally represent male energy. Female energy is represented by the hexahedron, a square. The dodecahedron is the number of life. Three male plus two female – variations of the pentagon."

"It's obvious why you got a medal for research. I think I read that the colour purple is linked to dignity and respect."

"Where did you read that? The colour supplement in a Sunday tabloid? I'm talking quantifiable scientific evidence," she said.

So what's with the dead cats?

Her sitting room was crammed with purple cats, some in fabric, some porcelain. There was one fashioned from matchsticks and painted a lurid shade of violet. Another had had a tussle with a taxidermist and lost. The creature sat atop a purple satin cushion and glared at me from a glass box.

"I don't dissect cats if that's what you're thinking," she said.

"Even I know physicists deal with the nebulous stuff," I replied.

"I'm allergic. No cats in the house."

"Collecting replicas is the next best thing?" I asked. She didn't smile.

I tried again. "A kind of hobby maybe?"

"Okay, my hobby, sort of. I grow lavender and distil the oil."

I didn't speak. I couldn't see the connection or a way forward.

"Afraid I dipped out of chemistry too," I replied at last. "My sister loves lavender. Says it's the best. She collects lavender soap wherever she travels. French lavender, English lavender, Portuguese lavender."

"Okay, related. But different varieties, different properties,"

118

she warned. "Just because they are related doesn't mean they should grow together – unhealthy, unnatural – not okay."

Was this a coded message on sibling friendship?

"I don't think Belinda plans to grow any lavender," was all I could manage.

"Okay," she said and with that she picked up a knitted purple cat, faded by its sunlit position on the window sill. She unzipped the creature's rump and pulled out a shoe-shaped, piece of mauve gauze filled with dried lavender.

"For Belinda, *quantum in me fuit.*"

"Thanks. I'm not sure quantum physics is quite her thing. But she'll love the smell and really appreciate the thought."

"Quantum is Latin for how much," Rosalie corrected me. "The saying is not from physics. It means I have done my best. Okay?"

As a timely end to an interview it probably was!

Now, of course, I can see why Rosalie Curtis might have been a suspect in the stalking and the stabbing that followed the panto debut. The police were curious about her caricature in my study. They wanted to know if I saw her as a devil figure.

"Frilly collars and hooves maketh more a satyr," I replied, taking their blank stares as confirmation that the average bobby still didn't study Greek.

Everyone in the pantomime had a history. There was Alice, the sweet veggie gardener who grew poisonous beans and cultivated wannabe stalkers in cyberspace. A promiscuous leading lady, Scheherazade, with a clandestine penchant for lovers and exotic settings. Rosalie, an emeritus professor of physics pining with unrequited lust for feet and females. Just three from a cast and crew that embraced half the village. The histories collided from time to time, not always agreeably. Who would match and catch a killer?

But it took Doris Dawes to illustrate the parallel universes of village fiction and fact when she proclaimed after the funeral in the pub, "It's not rocket science. I know we know who done it. It's like teaching cricket to foreigners. You might have seen what happened but you still need to understand why."

Wyeway was stumped.

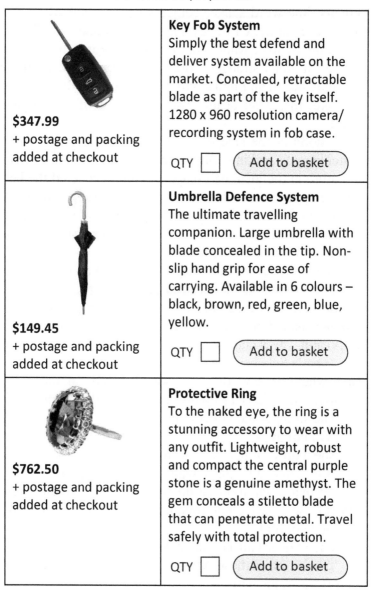

Key Fob System
Simply the best defend and deliver system available on the market. Concealed, retractable blade as part of the key itself. 1280 x 960 resolution camera/ recording system in fob case.

$347.99
+ postage and packing added at checkout

QTY ☐ (Add to basket)

Umbrella Defence System
The ultimate travelling companion. Large umbrella with blade concealed in the tip. Non-slip hand grip for ease of carrying. Available in 6 colours – black, brown, red, green, blue, yellow.

$149.45
+ postage and packing added at checkout

QTY ☐ (Add to basket)

Protective Ring
To the naked eye, the ring is a stunning accessory to wear with any outfit. Lightweight, robust and compact the central purple stone is a genuine amethyst. The gem conceals a stiletto blade that can penetrate metal. Travel safely with total protection.

$762.50
+ postage and packing added at checkout

QTY ☐ (Add to basket)

The Pantomime: Centre of the Edge

For me, the word stalker conjures up associations of hats and deer hunting. Or of deviant behaviour and fear. Or of a maladjusted man whose mother got it wrong. It does not suggest a pretty stranger; young and gothic clad, sitting in the audience of an English village pantomime. But make no mistake; that Thai beauty was in pursuit of her English beast.

I stood at the side of the village hall, near the front, watching and making notes. I had my commission to write a feature in the local newspaper. I commandeered the best vantage point to see who was attending the opening night of *Snow White* and to hear all the gossip. Not surprisingly, my brother-in-law, aka the Toad Prince, was chatting up the exotic newcomer beside him.

"Are you new to the village?" I heard him ask.

The woman shook her head but then directed her gaze to study the cast biographies listed in the programme. The woman had failed to recognise him as a face from television. I was chuffed!

"That's Scheherazade, our Leading Lady," Toad Prince said when he saw that she was focused on the star's photograph. "She's a step up from the usual am-dram."

The stranger did not comment.

"On holidays?"

She didn't lift her eyes to answer.

"First time at a village panto?" he tried again.

"Is that a variation on do you come here often?" said Doris Dawes, swivelling round in her squeaking seat. Take no notice of him."

The Stalker half-nodded but did not speak.

"She's one of those Asian girls. Won't speak English," said Boris to his wife.

"Do you think she's a mail order bride?" Doris replied.

The stranger massaged the large red stone in the ring on the third finger of her right hand. I think I saw her lips twitch.

"It's a dramatic statement against such a delicate hand," commented the Toad Prince with genuine admiration. "Looks dangerous and exciting. Not many women could carry off a ring like that."

I have to hand it to him. He never gives up on the charm offensive. The woman stopped caressing her ring. She turned her head and stared into his eyes.

Was that a half smile or sneer she gave him?

The Toad Prince ran his fingers through his thick, blonde curls. Had she unnerved him or was he miffed by her disinterest?

Ten gold stars to her.

"Is your wife coming then?" Doris asked him.

"Of course Belinda will be here," he smiled.

Doris's interrogation was interrupted by a young girl barging her way along the rows of empty chairs to where Belinda's husband and the Stalker sat.

"Oh I can't believe it's you," she gushed.

"It is," he said, switching into public performance mode. "What can I do for you?"

"Oh gosh, really... I wanted to ask a favour," the girl said.

"Her and the rest," said Doris to Boris. "No shame these days. I blame the mothers."

"If I can, I certainly will," replied the Toad Prince.

The young girl blushed.

"I'm thinking of auditioning for television," she blurted.

"Good luck."

"My family and friends think I've got a chance."

"I'm sure you do. Pretty girls are always in with a chance."

"No... I mean... well thanks. But I've got talent as well."

"Helps. It's very competitive out there."

"I won first prize in the Eisteddfod."

"That's good."

"Do you want to know what for?"

"I'm sure you're going to tell me."

"I won first prize for the under eighteen Bible reading and second prize for singing and tap dancing to *Somewhere over the Rainbow*."

"Congratulations. It's a good song."

"I brought along my prize certificate to show you... just in case you were here of course."

"Of course. So where would you like me to autograph it? Seeing that I'm here."

"Err... I'm not sure my Dad would want you to write on the certificate. It's the original. He's going to put it in a frame in our lounge. He's got a wall reserved for me. Start of my wall of fame, he says."

"Well I thought you wanted me to do you a favour?"

"I do. You might think it's a bit cheeky."

"I like cheeky."

"Could you help me with my audition piece? I could come round to your place anytime you like."

Boris and Doris Dawes swivelled, eye brows raised, to regard the local wannabe. So did a number of other audience members. My sister's husband took the girl's hand in his and stage whispered, "Talk to me after the show. I'll see what I can arrange"

Boris nudged Doris. Doris kicked Boris back. The Stalker fondled her ring, watched and waited. Another drama started in the audience before the curtain parted.

Doris leapt from her seat and called out to the short, middle-aged man strutting down the centre aisle of chairs.

"Oooeee, Director! Director, here."

She pointed to the Draylon-covered club chair positioned centre front. A large, hand painted piece of calligraphy perched on the chair arm with the word DIRECTOR. Harry Heil, the dapper figure in his British racing green cord trousers, removed the sign and nestled into his seat. He seemed content that his arrival had merited attention. Numbers of people congregated around Harry, shaking his hand, congratulating him on what was to come, eager to jockey position in the night's posse of fame and acclaim. Frank, from lighting, shuffled through the hall avoiding eye contact with anyone. He had a large rucksack slung across his left shoulder.

"I hope there's no home brew in that bag," commented Boris to Doris.

"Eh Frank, you planning to raise the roof this year?" boomed a voice from the audience.

Frank looked to the floor and stepped up his passage through the hall to a mild jog.

"Uncalled for," said Doris to Boris. "You've checked, haven't you? No mechanical apparatus?"

"It's just a bit of banter," said Boris.

"I don't call last year's insurance claim a bit of anything," responded Doris.

"It was fun though," confided Boris. "We did have a laugh when the beanstalk hit the sprinkler system."

"I didn't find it funny then. I don't find it in the slightest bit amusing now."

"Enough said, luv," said Boris to Doris.

"Humph," grunted Doris.

There was a commotion at the back of the hall as a number of people entered together. A figure pushed through them, sprinted down the hall and disappeared behind the curtains on the stage.

"Another late delivery," someone commented. People within hear shot laughed good-naturedly.

"Mr Nells, village postman," commented the Toad Prince to the Stalker. "He plays the back half of the cow."

Boris turned and explained to the Thai stranger.

"There is always a cow in our pantomime. Mr Nells is always the back half. Has been for twenty years."

"In our Snow White the cow juggles... very well in fact," Doris added.

The stranger looked blank. Juggling cows were not part of the Thai stage tradition I imagined.

"Hello darling," my sister called to her husband. "Isn't it a wonderful turn out?" she shouted to the Director. "All seats for the show have been sold."

She waved to me. I crossed to where Belinda now stood beside her husband.

"I won't sit with you tonight," I said. "Better to write my review from the back row. See you both after the show."

I left Belinda to deal with her smarm-charm husband and the intriguing Thai woman beside him.

"Foolish man," Doris said to Belinda. "How can he hear everyone from back there? The Fifth Sheep can't baa further than the third row to save her life."

"Perhaps my brother-in-law sees that as a blessing," commented Belinda's husband. "You may have to join him, my sweet, we're short of chairs."

Doris and Boris eyed the Toad Prince with hostility.

"Oh please," said the Thai outsider in perfect English, "take mine. I was keeping it warm until you arrived."

There was complete silence. Even Boris and Doris were speechless. Belinda's husband recovered first.

126

"There's a party after the performance," he said. "At The Turk. Come join us."

"It's mostly couples," snapped Doris and turned back to face the stage.

The stranger nodded and stood up. She glided elegantly to the end of the row. She walked to the back of the hall and looked around. When she saw me she inclined her head. I beckoned to indicate that there was a spare seat beside me. I noted with satisfaction that my brother-in-law did not look pleased.

"Mr Nolan, acting local hack," I said. "I get to do the review of opening night. It'll be biased of course. My sister Belinda wrote the script."

The woman acknowledged my statement but did not speak. She opened her programme at the page of cast photographs.

"You know our Leading Lady?" I asked.

"I know of her," the stranger replied.

"Met her in Thailand?" I ventured. The woman shook her head.

"Ah the joys of an Internet reputation," I suggested. "None of us are safe."

The woman smiled politely. End of conversation. The lights dimmed. The curtains opened. The pantomime began. The Leading Lady, framed by ten sheep performing the Can-Can in Wellingtons, foot perfect and whistling in unison, commanded centre stage. The audience burst into applause as the pantomime cow roller-bladed onto stage and juggled over-sized plastic apples, attached by elastic to the cow horns and tail. Within thirty seconds there was a mishmash of tangled plastic and elastic looped around cow appendages.

"Vive la moving parts!" shouted someone in the audience.

"Up udder and away," added another.

127

On stage, the lights dimmed and seven tap dancing trees shuffled forward to form a semi-circle around the Leading Lady. On cue their right hands circled and tapped their headdresses. Batteries were activated. Seven papier-mâché dwarves were illuminated. The audience erupted with cheers.

"Bravo," shouted Boris. Doris stood and bowed in the darkened hall acknowledging the loud applause for her efforts in costume engineering.

The dancing trees continued to swirl around the stage with the little men bobbing precariously aloft. Snow White's question to the audience:

"Seven little men
Hi-hoing in the trees,
Shall I follow after,
And solve this myst-er-y?"

was answered with a cheer and a mix of comments unprintable in the local paper.

The exotic woman beside me seemed perplexed.

"Long story but it's village life at its best," I whispered. "The bold, the beautiful, and the bloody bumptious."

"It's not Shakespeare," she said.

"You've studied English drama?" I asked.

"In Thailand, we are encouraged to read widely. Our own traditions are supported by the best from the West," she explained.

"Shame we don't offer the same breadth of education," I replied. "Most of our lot couldn't name anything literary from Thailand, ancient or modern. Unless you count *The King and I*."

"Yul Brunner is hardly authentic," she protested.

"The arrogance of empire, the ignorance of affluence," I agreed.

After the funeral I remembered the woman acknowledged that comment with a half nod and full breath. And I also remember that her eyes never left her quarry on stage. She kept her hands folded in her lap. Her left thumb rested on the ruby stone of her ring.

With hindsight I wonder if this posture reassured her. The prick of the poison concealed within the ring's shimmer. The jagged precision of the stone. Was the Stalker grounded at the centre of the edge?

Hospitality Award for Excellence

2011

Awarded to

Hercules Asmizchovic
at the Turkey and Tree, Wyeway

for first class service, food and beverages

Herk: Zoots, Toots and Champagne Flutes

I reckoned the post-performance party at the Turkey and Tree would be a feast for a graphic story or two. I fancied myself as the ace reporter. After all a PhD does confirm that I know how to research... and drink... simultaneously. The village pub in Wyeway is a sixteenth century, oak beamed, roaring log fire, horse brasses and copper jugs, kind of place. Seventy people can snuggle together over a drink to chin wag. After *Snow White* the pub was crammed with at least a hundred die-hard party goers. I squeezed amongst the revellers who toasted papier-mâché dwarves, juggling bovines, tap-dancing trees and the ten sex-sus sheep.

"Zoots, toots and champagne flutes, let's drink to the dregs of life," chorused Herk, the publican and Scheherazade, the Leading Lady, as many of the cast joined in a final rendition of the pantomime theme song. Boris and Doris Dawes had arrived with Harry Heil, the Director. Harry was centre stage at the bar, shaking hands with whosoever. I took the obligatory photographs while the revellers could stand upright and before clothing was shed to gyrate on the miniscule dance floor in the corner. It was a pleasure to be a participant observer. I got paid to eavesdrop and drink for posterity.

"Well done, old bean," said Boris for the umpteenth time as he raised his glass to Harry.

"Thank heavens the premiere was an insurance-claim-free event," whispered Doris to me.

Boris regarded the throng with anticipation. His wife scowled. My guess was that Doris had resolved to exit early.

"Once more unto the bar, dear wife," Boris misquoted. "Let mine eyes drink the vision of loveliness over yonder," he remarked to me as he waved at Scheherazade.

"She looks like a tart," said Doris as the Leading Lady, in her Lurex sheath and high heeled, purple suede boots waved back to him.

"Nothing like dessert then to finish a good evening," I replied. Boris smiled at my pun.

"Just a small whiskey sour for me," Doris snapped to Boris. "Now that one's definitely a lesbian." Doris pointed towards the Stage Manager, Rosalie Curtis, whose gaze was fixed on the said purple boots of the Leading Lady.

"No way, luv," replied Boris. "Even Herk's got a bedtime story about Scheherazade. Hasn't he Nolan?"

"Couldn't possibly comment," I said.

"Why not?" said Doris.

"Press licence, my lips are sealed and all that," I lied.

"I don't mean the Leading Lady is queer," argued Doris. "I'm talking about the Stage Manager. Just look at how Rosalie's staring at Scheherazade's legs. Strange?"

"Every bugger in this pub is drooling over those pins!"

"Not you Boris, I trust?"

"Too busy looking at her boobs, luv. Come on, lighten up, it's a party."

"What's that supposed to mean?"

"Nothing," Boris said.

"You mean it's Saturday night?" said Doris.

"Well it is, isn't?"

"Don't get any ideas," she warned and stormed off.

"HRT," Boris whispered to me.

The things a journalist learns.

Doris had headed towards the gaggle of Women's Institute members. I didn't follow. Rumour had it gynaecology and husband shredding was a favourite topic with that particular group of girls. Instead I Boris-watched. He headed in the opposite direction to his wife where the Toad Prince, my brother-in-law, was flirting with the mystery visitor from the Orient. Perhaps our Leading Lady had a rival for queen of the cast party?

Might get interesting.

I was about to cross the room but could not help overhearing my sister giggle with Herk, the publican.

"Come on Herk," Belinda goaded, "you promised, remember?"

"Yeah, when I was drunk."

"Well, you're sober enough to get the story out. Come on."

"No laughing – you promise?"

"Cross my heart and hope to die," Belinda promised.

"Don't die in here Belinda. Health and safety will shut me down."

"Well then, you have to tell me the story."

"Me Da," Herk began, "was a puny bloke. Bad asthmatic as a kid. Bullied at school. No hope with the girls. You get the picture?"

"So you were a test tube baby? Who was the sperm donor – a rugby forward?" smiled Belinda.

"Nah, Da joined the gym, discovered the coach had a direct line to a dodgy chemist, got a barrow load of steroids and da de da de da as they say."

"And your mum?"

"Daughter of the coach. He hailed from Czechoslovakia. Fled to Constantinople. She was a female shot putter training to be an Olympic gold medallist."

"Wow, did your mum go to the Olympic Games?"

"Nah, met me Da, got herself pregnant. They nicknamed her bump Hercules. I dropped out six months before team selection."

"Jolly bad timing for the team," consoled Belinda.

"You said it," Herk agreed.

"Could be worse. Your Dad might have been into

synchronised swimming and eloped with a cox. Imagine what sort of pub name you'd have to look for? Flipper up the Slipper? Kipper on the River?"

"I'd rather not," he laughed. "Hercules at the Turkey and Tree is bad enough."

"Herk you'll always be my knight at the Turk."

Herk looked over at Belinda's husband. He was kissing the hand of the Thai woman.

"You're a nice lady Belinda. You ever want to chuck that twat out, I'll be waiting."

"Don't hold your breath Herk. I love him, really, really love him."

"I figured that."

They watched the Leading Lady advance to the oak post against which the Toad Prince was leaning as he conversed with no-name exotica from Thailand.

"He can't help being beautiful," sighed Belinda.

"Like you can't stop being sweet," said Herk.

"Perfect combination then, isn't it?"

Deciding it was time to do my civic duty and rescue our foreign visitor from the clutches of the Toad, I left eavesdropping and began to navigate my way across the room. Half way there I bumped into the Leading Lady.

"Who is the unknown quantity?" asked Scheherazade as she noticed the Toad Prince and his companion.

"No idea. I thought she might be one of yours," I replied.

"I don't know all the prostitutes in Bangkok."

"She's not a working girl. Fascinated by you though."

"Aren't they all darling?"

"You're a shameless shag, you know that?"

"As they say, like attracts like."

With that, she turned and left me in search of new adoration. So the mystery visitor remained just that. Maybe the Toad Prince had found out more about her with his smarm charm. My attempts had been a waste of time. Charmingly polite but elusive, I hadn't got a jot of useful information from any of my questions to her when she sat beside me during the pantomime. But she had seemed as fixated on the Leading Lady as the rest of the audience. It didn't dawn on me that there might be a connection through Scheherazade's professional life. No doubt Belinda, the gold medallist in English literature, could have quoted William Congreve to remind me

Heaven has no Rage, like Love to Hatred turned,
Nor Hell a Fury, like a Woman scorned.[4]

Suddenly, Frank, the hero in lighting, gave a piercing whistle and the noise subsided. It was time for the speeches. The Fifth Sheep, Alice Sweet, had changed from her mal fitting costume into a flouncy, red skirt that shone even in the dim lighting of the pub. She fluttered a floral fan in front of her sweaty face and glowed adoringly at Frank. A double for Scarlett O'Hara she was not.

"Another great night?" boomed Frank.

"Oh yes it is," the group responded.

"It's time for the Oscars," said Frank.

"Oh no it's not," applauded the group.

"Oh yes it is," said Frank, "and the next person to interrupt gets to buy us all a drink."

The crowd went silent. Frank began his list of thank-you-folks, starting with Belinda, the script writer, then Harry, the Director, and ending with the Village Hall Committee. Boris and Doris beamed with pride as they presented Harry with his present from the cast. Harry's face was somewhere between a grimace and a Mona Lisa smile as he graciously accepted the folding chair. Rescued from

---

[4] William Congreve: *The Mourning Bride*: 1697

a skip, the chair had been lovingly repaired, painted British racing green, re-slung in multi-coloured patchwork, the word DIRECTOR embroidered across the back of the chair, with a matching bag into which it could be folded and carried to rehearsals for years to come. Rosalie Curtis, the Stage Manager, presented Belinda with a large bouquet of flowers – purple tulips.

"My final duty is to announce the award for this year's Turkey and Tree show stopper. Herk, hand me the trophy," demanded Frank.

"Stuff the turkey!" the throng responded on cue. Herk handed Frank an oversized child's toy. It was a gaudy, fabric turkey with a collar around its neck studded with the names of former winners.

Herk held the trophy above his head and said, "This year's award goes to Doris Dawes and her team for their creations – the dazzling, all dancing, dwarves."

I made my notes... *seven little papier-mâché chaps... sitting on the tops of headdresses... worn by the tap dancing trees.* After all those heated arguments about dwarves on stage at the script read through, a will and a way had been found. With a bit of art and craft, all things were possible in our village politics.

Then the party proper commenced. The music rose a few too many decibels. The lights were lowered. Frank and his techies settled down for an all-night drinking session. Cowering in a corner, the Fifth Sheep cast tearful glances at Frank, punctuated by frenetic surveillance of the crowds. Was Alice hapless or hopeful that her cyberspace admirer, Rhett Butler, number 532 from Reading, had turned up to see her perform? I also noted a scowl on the face of the Stage Manager as she studied Alice's footwear.

That's when I heard the scream.

I'd know Belinda's voice anywhere. I looked around.

Belinda was half way up the staircase behind the bar. Those stairs led to Herk's private quarters and the rooms he offers for bed and breakfast.

"An ambulance, an ambulance, we need an ambulance!"

There was mayhem in the pub. People, drunk-dancing and shout-singing to the best of the 70's music, gyrated oblivious to Belinda's distress call. Herk leapt onto the bar and waved his arms. Many of the dancers assumed he was joining in the dancing and cheered. Some moved to form a line. They put their hands on the nearest piece of anatomy and Conga-ed in front of the bar and out the door of the pub into the village. I saw the Thai visitor heading towards the Leading Lady, followed by the Director and the Stage Manager. They all jockeyed for first place, to stand behind Scheherazade and put their arms around her waist in the dancing queue. The Thai won. She held fast to the Lurex sheath. Not to be thwarted, the Stage Manager pushed the Director in front of her and then barged in front of Scheherazade. The Leading Lady threw her arms around the Stage Manager. Everyone smiled and sang.

Stairway to a personal heaven.

Moments later I saw Scheherazade stumble and pull away from the winding throng.

Those damn high heels are lethal.

I shouted, "Scheherazade you'll break a leg."

By the time the ambulance arrived, the tableaux in the pub was worthy of the best cliff hanger in a soap opera. Belinda was sobbing as she cradled her husband's head in her lap. I stared, humiliated, as Shirley Nolan descended the staircase, aware that her less-than-discrete rendezvous with Belinda's husband would be public knowledge. But my wife's eyes were not on me. She headed towards a dimly-lit corner of the room. There, sprawled on the floor, was Scheherazade, half hidden in the shadows, her dress slashed to the right of her waist. Rolling her over, a stain appeared. It looked like blood. Like a banshee, my wife wailed, "Oh God, Scheherazade's hurt. I think my sister's been stabbed."

GONE with the WIND
…live the dream … live the dream … live the dream…

Scarlett must be gone with the wind

	Re: Show over By sweet and sexy Snow White >>> 1700 Adieu my lovelies, 'tis time for Scarlett Snow White to exit stage right forever. Seven vertically challenged men of the forest may mourn the decision. Alas recent events show my path must lead to new adventures in wonderland. Arise, Lady Alice of the garden.
	Re: Show over By Rhett Butler 189 >>> 1725 My dear, A loss for your loyal admirers. A gain for the garden. A rose beyond all others will blossom forever more.
	Re: Show over By Rhett Butler 532 >>> 1750 Honey child I is gonna ride into the sunset with tears in ma eyes for ma scarlet chickadee! But ya ever decide ya want a man to get his hands dirty… ya just holla and I'll come running.

Re: Show over
By Reverend Butler >>> 1755

Bless you Scarlett, retire in peace, may your garden be Eden and see you in the next world.

Re: Show over
By Rhett Butler 222 >>> 1803

The lady is judged a disappointment to all concerned. On stage today, gone with the wind tomorrow.

Re: Show over
By Rhett Butler 58 >>> 1824

Fly me to the moon you star of cyberspace and stage.

Re: Show over
By Rhett Butler 437 >>> 1846

Amigo, south of the border, you can garden in my hacienda any time you want.

Re: Show over
By sweet and sexy Snow White >>> 1902

Frankly my dears I do give a damn! Parting is such sweet sorrow. Farewell and travel safe. P.S. Watch out for the bad apple!!!

Nosey Nolan: Who Stole Tomorrow?

When I said "None of us is safe," I wasn't trying to be prophetic. It was a flippant remark to a beautiful Thai stranger sat beside me at our village pantomime. But timing is critical whether you are a journalist with deadlines to meet, a stalker on a mission to murder, or God himself coming to collect his next mortal instalment. Time was not on my side when I was commissioned to compose an obituary in addition to a front page feature for the *County Chronicle*.

The hat trick, my own fairytale-not, was an attempt to sanitise the complexities of family relationships. I titled it *Women of Wyeway*, kept it locked inside my computer, filed under New Directions.

> *Once upon a time, there lived a plump princess called Belinda Beloved who wrote plays for the people in a village called Wyeway. The villagers lauded her efforts to keep them entertained. In return she adored her loyal community. But above all she loved the frog prince who plopped out of the television and chose to live in her pond. Most of her village suspected he was a toad in spouse clothing. Belinda believed he was her soul mate in a happy ever after lifetime.*

My sister Belinda is still beyond reach, so deep is the grave of her mourning. Tom, the toad prince, her husband, is dead and buried. His body lay for two days in the hospital mortuary on a slab of stainless steel, sliced open to find answers, re-stitched for disposal. The pathologist completed the autopsy. I awaited the official result before submitting my column. I certainly didn't intend to praise him. But I did need to present the facts before we buried him.

141

Belinda Beloved has a brother, the Nosey Nolan, who keeps his eyes open and ears alert to stories that a princess may not choose to hear.

Upstairs at the hospital, in intensive care, Scheherazade, the pantomime's Leading Lady, who enchanted young and old alike, remains in a coma.

Scheherazade is a Sleeping Beauty with a difference. The prognosis is that she will not tell stories for some time, possibly not for a thousand and one nights. Sinbad, Aladdin, Ali Baba, seven dwarves and her many admirers must wait and pray that she wakes up. Neither a kiss from me or her sister, Shirley, will help.

I can't remember much detail of the scenario. The doctors tell me this is a normal response to trauma. Everyone wants to give advice.

"Counselling might help."

"Focus on the good things in your life."

"Not all people are bad."

Platitudes, platitudes… sometimes bad things happen that good people do not even dream about.

I do recall that on the night Herk, the publican at the Turkey and Tree, telephoned the emergency services. He ordered everything on wheels and everyone in uniform. My brother-in-law, Tom Prince, was dead but there was no blood. Scheherazade, my sister-in-law, was alive with a blood stain on the side where her Lurex dress was ripped. My sister Belinda and Shirley, my wife, were hysterical. The paramedics darted between the bodies.

Rosalie Curtis, the Stage Manager, went into control mode and ordered the onlookers out of the pub.

Harry Heil, still acting as Director, led the group outside in a prayer and a song.

Alice Sweet reverted from Scarlett the harlot to the Fifth Sheep and bleated relief. Then she threw herself at Frank promising to protect him.

"Why do I need protecting?" asked a confused Frank.

"It's all my fault," Alice cried. "Rhett Butler number 532 from Reading is a stalker."

"Who is this Butler fellow?" said Frank who then promptly vomited.

"A stalker! A stalker!" shouted Doris Dawes. It wasn't clear if she considered this snippet to be a threat or a promise.

Boris tried to frog-march his wife away from the unpleasantness of it all, advising, "Best not get mixed up in other folks' mess, luv."

Doris refused to budge and shouted to the throng, "Anyone got a camera? Or one of those thing-a-me-bobby phones with a video? The television news will pay for pictures of this. We'll be famous."

Boris, as Chair of the Village Hall Committee, went into meltdown. Doris smoothed her hair and snapped at Herk, "Are you insured for this?"

I don't remember exactly what Herk replied but it wasn't polite.

Snow White, our sleeping beauty off the stage, has succumbed to the poison of jealousy. Her reputation as the village bike has been dwarfed by the news of her stabbing. Not by a wicked stepmother but an avenging wife. The Leading Lady has been caught out having an affair with a

143

doctor married to a Thai woman. The Leading
Lady and the medic work together for a charity.
It rehabilitates the victims of sex tourism in
Thailand. Love and lust in Paradise has morphed
into a living nightmare. The king is an adulterer.
His lover is in need of a life support machine and
not a kiss to wake up. His queen is wanted for
attempted murder. There will be no fairytale
ending.

The pathologist rang me with the autopsy results.
The Toad Prince would not claim any heroic headlines.
He died innocently – an aneurysm. I envisaged the
headlines:

Bonking my wife blew his brains!

Mr Nolan, journalist cum academic cum sleuth, puzzles
who's up who in his family panto.

Oh no can it be true?

Nolan's wife was in flagrante delicto with the husband
of Nolan's sister.

Oh yes it can!

Now wouldn't that have made great copy?

Maybe for a national tabloid. But for the local
newspaper I settled for an obituary that simply stated:

TELEVISION STAR DROPS DEAD
AT PANTOMIME PARTY.

Police speculation about the stabbing of my sister-in-
law is that our exotic visitor had poison concealed in the
dazzling, stiletto jewel of her ring. None of us can
remember the Thai woman, stalking away unnoticed in the
mist and madness.

"Enter as a whirlwind, depart as an ant," I recall saying
to Scheherazade over an illicit lunch.

I filed my feature with the *County Chronicle.*

The County Chronicle
News and views on what's happening locally

Stalker stabs stage star

Mystery surrounds the attack on Scheherazade, the Leading Lady, at The Turkey and Tree. Following a sell-out performance of the pantomime, *Snow White and the Seven Dwarves*, the cast and friends celebrated at the local pub.

Around 11 p.m. an ambulance was called to attend to Scheherazade. She remains in a critical but stable condition. Publican, Hercules Asmizchovic, said, "It's a terrible shock. Nothing like this has ever happened in our village."

A hospital spokesperson announced that Scheherazade was in intensive care with renal failure and blood poisoning.

Doctors confirmed that a puncture wound was located on the right side of the patient's kidney. The wound had traces of the toxic substance, Ricin, a by-product of processing castor beans into castor oil. The poison became famous in the "umbrella murder" of Soviet dissident Georgi Markov in 1978. Markov was stabbed with an umbrella that injected a pellet into his leg. He died three days later.

Police have revealed that they visited Wyeway's allotments following reports that gardeners have been cultivating castor beans. They have also confirmed that they would like to speak to an Oriental woman, possibly from Thailand, who attended the pantomime and party after in the Turkey and Tree pub. However police declined to comment on whether she is the wife of an English doctor working for a charity in Bangkok.

Reliable sources say that the Leading Lady is director of a charity that works to rehabilitate prostitutes working in the tourist area of Patpong.

As Scheherazade fights for her life, her sister Mrs Shirley Nolan prays at her hospital bedside...

Is there a man in the moon? Is he listening to my prayers?

After the surreal funeral of my brother-in-law and a grim vigil at the hospital for my sister-in-law, I arrived home to find a myriad of treasures sitting at my back door. Frank, from lighting, had left a whole case of his home brew. There was a container of pumpkin soup from the Fifth Sheep with a sticker guaranteeing its organic origins (and a handwritten note assuring me that any castor oil

146

plants on the allotment had been uprooted and burnt on police recommendation). Boris and Doris Dawes had made a With Sympathy card conveying their thoughts on the horror and sadness of it all.

Herk sent a book of Turkish quotations addressed to Belinda, Shirley and me. Inside the front cover he had written:

> *"Gönül ne kahve ister ne kahveh ane, gönül sohbet ister." (One neither desires coffee nor a coffee house. One desires to talk with others, coffee is merely an excuse.* Turkish proverb*).*

An anonymous delivery from I-know-who revealed the latest tenant-in-waiting. A jolly green gnome with a yellow hat smiled in sympathy as he held a red fishing net containing seven dwarves. I said a silent thank you as I placed the kitsch statue beside its fellow friends. Those gnomes flagged up the absurdities and beauty of a community where all contributions matter.

And finally, tied to the door knob was a bunch of lavender from the Stage Manager. A mauve ribbon was attached with a note, "Not okay today but tomorrow will be better."

It had better be.

So as I sat and reflected on my return from Australia, the months of village life with its annual pantomime, its cycle of births, deaths and marriages, I too felt moved to offer up a prayer or three.

Forgive my promiscuous wife. Help Shirley Nolan to accept her infertility. Help her reconcile with Scheherazade, her sister, who chose to abort a cargo of lust. Let my wife respect me for my commitment and cuddles.

Comfort my sister-in-law and grieving sister. Let Scheherazade and Belinda find peace in their time. Grant them a future life with partners that deserve their beauty and respect their bodies.

And please Mr Man in the Moon remember me. Please give me something more than second hand stories of other people's loves and losses. I want to bowl people over with initiative; stump them with originality; field optimism. I don't want to die asking who stole tomorrow. I want to be a player and not the reserve.

I like happy endings.

LITERARY LINKS

Something Sweet

Between you, me and the printing press there's not a lot I don't know about women. Seven million females who speak thirty different languages can vouch for me. Of course I haven't had the personal pleasure (that'd be beyond even your average adolescent's wet dream) but the collective experiences of my clones stand me in wise words.

"You wouldn't read about it!"

"Stranger than fiction."

I've heard them all, from Alaska to Zanzibar, in Chinese to Xhosa, out of the mouths of crones to Fräuleins. I try to be fair and impartial but like all principles it never quite works out that way. There's always the odd female reader that touches you. Beyond speculation, Ruth, Judy, Lauren, Francis and Amani confounded me and became the five big. Right up there with those African icons – elephant, rhinoceros, lion, leopard and buffalo.

But KJ is the legend. She's really, really special.

Well naturally I hear you sigh, "Kesia Jaskins is your birth mother."

That she is. But I know that you know that not every woman knows, loves or even likes her biological mum. I love KJ and KJ loves me, full circle, no genetic connection. She and me, it's been a volatile relationship. From conception to independence, we've crawled, cheered and cried together, through the pages, amongst the punctuation, words fastened together. It's a journey of life from which all readers can empathise and learn.

Sometimes KJ and I are one. Though inseparable, we present different faces in public. But don't be lulled into thinking we don't share the responsibility. Call KJ a godless whore, it makes me a literary strumpet. Laugh at her jokes, smile on my page. Listen to her voice, eat my words. Our link's symbiotic. Sometimes I want to ask her, who feeds who?

Take the launch for example. KJ and me under the glare; we looked pristine. Crisp, white, straight-spined both of us were objects of desire and esteem. Except that KJ had an itch in a place that she daren't scratch in public. Grimacing, she hoped it would go away. Or at least dissipate its urgency so that she could concentrate hard enough for long enough on her three hundred admirers seated in front of the lectern. Loyal fans assembled for my launch – her new book – *An Appetite for Words*. Faithful readers knew the drill. Kesia would set the context of her writing, read a passage or two, address familiar questions from the well-meaning audience and then sign copies. Later we would go back to her hotel room. Then she could scratch away. Meanwhile her supporters would carry a personalised volume back to their own abodes. The media would circulate the plaudits. Her publisher would sleep long and dream well about profits.

Kesia has had ten good years since her dipsy-tipsies. That's how I describe when her life unravelled. Before that she served her time as an upwardly mobile journalist after a stint as a copywriter.

But I digress. Back to the launch and when the lights dimmed, the applause faded. She gripped me hard, smiled, her eyes casing the expectant faces before her, and began: "Confucius said that before you embark on a journey of revenge, you should dig two graves. One for your quarry. One for yourself. When I started this book, some fifteen years ago, I was angry, depressed and determined to right some wrongs. Wrongs of the world in general and pain particular to me. At that time I was a journalist. The pressure to file a weekly column ensured a flow of words on topics as diverse as the ethics of intelligence (comedy) to the politics of nail varnish (tragedy). It seemed too easy to write a rant with a witty or pithy punch line. But when I set about flinging words against the canker of my existence, the language ran away and hid behind the self-deception that was my life. When you're dead inside, the pulse of promise stops beating. The world becomes murky. Nothing blossoms in darkness. There is no formula to calculate nothingness.

"My jottings from that period were half cocked. The proposed title of this book was dreary. I put the missive away for another time. End of. Begin afresh.

"Nothing like an editor to kick start your vocabulary and challenge your wallowing. Nothing like assignments and deadlines to make you focus. Nothing like sifting detail to explain an overview and captivate readers. By the time I rescued my crusade project from the back of the filing cabinet, I knew that peace, not revenge, was the healthier option."

KJ paused, stroked my cover, and surveyed her listeners. I know she is constantly surprised by the range of her readers. Her publisher called it her Coca-Cola appeal. At first she took it as an insult. Fizzy? Frivolous? Vapid?

"No," the publisher explained, "Coca-Cola – the real thing, universal, all inclusive, delightfully addictive."

Personally I thought he was a prat and a soft drink-swigging parasite but KJ rates him highly. Writers might be talented on paper but from what I see in bookshops and libraries you have to wonder sometimes about their reality. But before I go completely tangential, let me return to the launch.

In the front row I saw two stalwarts of her book signings – Juleigh Brisbane and Robyn Grammar. One is a grandmother from the Scottish highlands, the other a fitness teacher in Brighton. Juleigh cooks the best ever lavender shortbread. Robyn makes her own body lotion from home grown geraniums. Both brought their votive offerings to exchange with a signed copy of KJ's book. She regarded it as one of the real pleasures in the circus of book selling. Over the years Kesia has met many of her devoted readers. The Juleigh's and the Robyn's of her world are keen to offer their stories to an author who's willing to listen.

KJ was prepared for the most frequently asked questions, one of which was whether her characters were real people. Kesia always says yes, kind of. Not one real person of course. She doesn't want to get sued for defamation or share the royalties. But each and every character in her book combines the best, the worst, the most interesting and the dullest of experiences that she has encountered in her forty five years.

I laughed at the story about Brian from Kennington, who she suffered in Thailand. He still holds the record for the person most likely to bore her to death. According to KJ she had been stuck with Brian in a small boat for six long hours as she island-hopped from Ko Samui. The outboard engine failed. Fuel leaked. Reinforcements and repairs had to be negotiated. The sun was hot. Brian liked to talk, a lot, without pause. A natural for *Mastermind* he told her. His topic was train travel. Kesia reckoned, at first, that she might glean some useful information on destinations and route variations. Appearing interested and asking a few questions turned out to be her major mistake. Brian did plan journeys for trains. Model trains that ran like clockwork around miles of tracks that could be laid and re-laid according to his lack of imagination, his plastic mountains, trees, lakes, and all manner of topography. KJ couldn't believe how many variations on here we go round the mountain in Thomas the Tank Engine were possible. She did know that after five hours, jumping overboard and taking her chances with the sharks offered the only relief. The welcome arrival of a marine mechanic armed with spanners, diesel and a very loud tape player changed her fate. Never had she so enjoyed *The Best of Blondie*.

KJ has used real names of fans for her characters. She likes to think of it as a reward. A kind of loyalty card. Buy half a dozen, first edition novels and get a ticket for the literary lottery that is marketing today. Her publisher suggested that she should find ways to connect directly with her readers. Kesia was horrified at first. Not couch casting? Could work for her if the candidates looked like George Clooney. But otherwise...

"No," the publisher laughed, "get your readers on side. Make it personal, up close and let them feel the pain, the thrill, the tension in your writing."

I thought the advice sounded rather melodramatic, akin to being someone's birth partner and pre-empting contractions. Fortunately she talked to her cousin who worked in public relations. The cousin came up trumps and suggested a competition. Readers could post in a name for a character with a reason justifying the selection of that name, all in twenty words.

"Brief but brilliant," said her publisher.

"Great idea," agreed the books editor of the Sunday tabloid who featured the competition.

Bad idea... KJ received fifteen hundred entries... major disruption to the writing schedule. The majority had posted their own names and signed the disclaimer that guaranteed she could not face legal action for whatever characteristics she assigned to her real life people. I was truly sobered to see how many Helen Jameses there were in the world.

KJ compiled another list. One that lived in the top drawer of her desk. The list of those unlikely names was an antidote for writer's block and the glums. Did it matter if Honor Dagworthy who married George Heap and took his name was real or not? It made me chuckle.

"As many of you will know from the advance publicity," KJ continued to her audience, "this book is a collection of my newspaper columns during those difficult months, fifteen years ago. Some were published, others not. The words reflected a milestone in my life. Love. Cause and effect. Benefits and costs. It's a kind of accounting handbook. Not about lovers, numbers or how to organise affairs. More about feelings and how to decipher meaning."

KJ paused and squeezed me tight. I imagined that her itch had re-surfaced. I willed the irritation to oblivion. But she breathed deeply, raised me to head height and bowed her face towards my pages.

"Ruth," she muttered.

In the seats kept for late comers I caught the gaze of a black woman sitting to the far left in the back row. KJ had not seen Ruth Watling enter. I knew that this woman was like her itch, hovering under cover, ready to make a presence felt, just when KJ didn't need it. Déjà vu.

So Ruth had come back into her life. Would she ask KJ for a personal inscription?

So Sajud must know. Mustn't he?

What would KJ sign: To Sajud with… With what? Love, hate or blood?

You Judas!

KJ lowered me to reading level. I saw her look away when the Ruth woman half smiled.

Whew, I thought, crisis over. As if.

KJ began again.

"So, as I sifted and mixed, strained and blended experience and memory, the book began to resemble a cookbook. Freshly picked moments of intimacy, a cracked

156

heart, two dollops of dreams, a melted moment. All the ingredients of a life listed and laid out in preparation. Mix the rawness of those ingredients with hindsight and bake in the moderate heat of middle age. What do you get? A mystery taste, with a little of something familiar and a hint of the exotic unnamed but with the promise of fresh delight to tempt your taste buds.

An Appetite for Words describes a period of eighteen months. A lot happened. I grew up. I tasted the world with all its juices, bitter and sweet, fragrant and foul. Real names have been changed to protect individuals. Yet the essence of the experience is detailed. Its legacy derailed my life and impacted on many others. And like all memories, there are sounds, smells and tastes that link time, place and face.

A shrewd bookseller will tell you that there is nothing like a good book. I hope that's how you'll rate my book. It is so much more than a mere collection of printed pages with my reflections on life and love. You'll find some favourite recipes from time to time – savour and enjoy."

KJ basked in the applause that followed.

I remained rigid with pride. MORE THAN, she said. I'm more than!

I didn't dare look to see if Ruth was staying to hear KJ read an extract. But I could tell her itch had resurfaced with a vengeance. KJ tightened her abs, thereby silently damning her body's insistence, opened my luscious covers and began to read in a clear voice from chapter one of *An Appetite for Words*:

> *Man does not live by food alone. Words can feed a soul hungry for sustenance, whet an appetite for laughter, tempt the taste buds of imagination, seduce with the suggestion of what is yet to be offered. Words and food are best served with*

157

careful preparation, consideration of flavour and a regard for strength. Sharing food and exchanging words are communal activities. They are forms of living art that display creativity, celebrate diversity, demonstrate ingenuity, provide harmony and offer frivolity. Words, like food, can nourish our bodies, stimulate our senses and satisfy our longing with the subtle flavours of innuendo.

When I was young I thought falling in love would be like eating a favourite curry. HE would be delicious to the eye, savoury to smell, hot to touch and spicy to taste. It was therefore a double-dip bruiser to discover love was more Big Mac (full-of-promise, soon cold, unfulfilling with a sour after-taste) than yummy-scrummy body fodder.

Judas was gourmet. Think chocolate. Not the three o'clock sugar-hit-kind of chocolate with its foil wrapper winking at you beside the till at the supermarket. Not the up-market brand of organic, impress the guests, after-dinner kind of stuff. Judas was the forbidden, the exotic, the exquisite, the stuff to make you salivate. He was dark, tempered to a high gloss, seductive and out of my league. But all women can admire perfection. Especially when it arrives gift wrapped. Judas came swathed in red silk wearing a dog collar.

Cocoa is shipped to London from West Africa. So are good Catholic sons training to be priests. When I met Judas, he was thirty and on track for ordination. I was pale and mildly interesting. He met his nemesis, Kesia Jaskins, the quintessential

158

English rose. Judas was intoxicated by the scent of the chase. He didn't see the thorns. My nubile flesh provided camouflage. Judas was doomed. From the heat of the passion I morphed into a beetroot.

Tempering chocolate ensures its finish is lustrous with that characteristic chocolate snap. But to temper chocolate like an expert, you have to make sure that it doesn't heat up or cool down too quickly. Restraint and time are the key words to get it looking at its best. Restraint and time are not part of the vocabulary of lovers. I glowed with longing and melted in lust. Judas was my dream lover. Body and soul, our insatiable appetites were perfectly matched.

The pregnancy was more chocolate bloom than Valentine delight. Just as unsightly, mould-like coating limits the shelf life of chocolates, Judas was caught short by my news. I expected a crisis of faith, some serious lamentation, a difficult interview with the church fathers. The box, unwrapped, revealed goods altered by improper handling.

Hail Marys must have worked for him. Judas tossed me aside. In due course he was ordained.

I blossomed into a single fat lump whose chocolate pudding condition appealed to neither family nor friends...

P.S. For those of you who aren't that quick I would like to clarify KJ's attempt at literary intrigue or anagram as she would call it. For Judas read Sajud, and Sajud equals Judas. I wouldn't like to comment on my other half's endeavours other than to suggest that words like subtle, simple and stupid might seem apt. But I would like to suggest that if you make her following recipe, which KJ listed as the embodiment of passion (comparing mere food to immortal words… please I ask you!) DON"T spill the crumbs on my pages. A serious sense of humour failure is assured from us both.

Something Sweet – Chocolate and Beetroot Cupcakes

150g cocoa powder
360g self-raising flour
500g raw sugar
500g cooked beetroot
6 large eggs
400ml corn oil
3 teaspoons vanilla extract
1 teaspoon nutmeg, grated

1. Sift the cocoa powder and flour into a large bowl.
2. Mix in the sugar and nutmeg.
3. Puree the beetroot in a food processor.
4. Add eggs, corn oil and vanilla extract.
5. Pour into the large bowl and mix thoroughly with the cocoa and flour.
6. Pour mixture into cupcake cases and bake in 180°C oven for 25 minutes or until cooked. Lift cases out of baking pan onto a wire rack and leave to cool. Dust with icing sugar, or top with a dollop of mascarpone and a physalis or berry.

Makes 24

Something Spicy

There are three things you need to know about Ruth Watling. Firstly, she's as black as the print on this page. Secondly, she has three indulgences – books, spicy coconut soup and silk knickers – in no particular order. Thirdly, she hates surprises.

Although I had heard the gory details of what I call Ruth Truth, I would not have expected things to develop the way they did. But that's women for you. Even an encyclopaedia wouldn't bet against those hormones.

When Ruth was seven her grandmother took her unexpectedly to visit her Auntie Maway in the women's hut. It turned out to be one hell of a surprise. Four women held her down. Auntie wielded the blade. Ruth passed out with the pain.

At fifteen, an Indian nun, under the guise of health care in the community, came to convert her West African village to Christianity.

"Ruth," said the nun, "that surprise has a well-documented name. It's called female genital mutilation. In many places people who give that sort of surprise get sent to prison."

Girls on surprise visits to Auntie Maway got to stay alone in a special hut for 30 days. On every one of those days Ruth was made to hobble to the women's beach, her legs buckling with the pain from the butchery and the chaffing of the hessian cloth that bound her thighs together.

"Sitting in salt water is good medicine," the old women told her.

They lied. It hurt. And in Ruth's case, the daily dunking did not stop infection. The legacy of Ruth's childhood surprise made her an adult control queen.

Her brother, Sajud smuggled bowls of spicy coconut

soup to the hut where she lay removed from her family, bleeding, frightened, stinking and feverish.

"I know it's your favourite," he said.

Ruth didn't stop to consider who made it for him to bring. He was her hero.

Coconuts were the wonder food in her part of Africa. The village drank its milk, cooked the fleshy inside of the shell, chewed the roots, wove the fibre into baskets, used the tree trunks for building houses, made fences from the leaf stalks, fashioned baskets, fishing tackle, mats and roofs from mature leaves. Sajud was an expert at tapping the tree and helped the men brew the sap into wine.

At school Ruth's teacher told coconut stories from around the world.

"In some parts of India, holy men give coconuts to women to help them have babies. In Bali, females are not allowed to touch them. The priests say women will become barren. On some South Pacific islands money is made from coconuts."

But to Ruth coconuts simply meant home, where she was loved and protected.

"Home is somewhere safe," she had told her teacher.

"Remember coconut palms can bear fruit after seven years and live for a hundred," her teacher said.

After her surprise, Ruth had a new plan.

"I don't plan to spend a century living in a place that violates women so openly," she told the nun. "As soon as I can, I'm leaving home, getting the hell out of my village, this state and my country. I'm heading north towards the promised land."

To Ruth, Mecca was London. The weather challenged but the city brimmed with women from everywhere, women who didn't rate genital mutilation as a prerequisite for marriage.

In time, her new life got better. Sajud left Africa and came to study. She had family, real flesh, matched blood. He studied God. She learnt about a hell where English doctors couldn't repair village surgery. Sajud loved to debate theological problems and philosophical theory. She preferred to deliver practical solutions for women in need. They shared good times and many bowls of spicy coconut soup through the English winters. And the discovery of free public libraries with thousands of books available kept brother and sister busy and informed.

Sajud ended up a soul-saving priest and a runaway father. Auntie's damage determined Ruth's path.

"You won't ever be able to have children," the gynaecologist said.

Ruth changed her African name to an easy English one. Missie Abagbe was dead. Long live Ms Ruth, director of a charity that campaigned against genital mutilation of women from anywhere.

"Dyecora Sumda," they called her.

The words meant circle of life. Women in need, women in pain, angry women, young, old, white, black, rich, poor, Ruth's circle welcomed any with a double X chromosome.

"What about men?" asked a friend. "You planning to get married to an Englishman or one of your own?"

"Nothing wrong with male company," Ruth replied.

But her life did not include men in any sexual sense.

"Ways of seeing do not change if the lens remains the same," she confided. "I could never expose my body to any man outside my culture. Too difficult, too different, too much baggage to explain."

"Then get that brother of yours to introduce you to someone African."

"No, I won't share a bed with a man who comes from a

culture where a woman has to be prepared in that way for marriage."

Silk knickers were Ruth's treat to her private parts. The ugliness and memories of childhood torture were encased, protected and caressed by the softest, most flimsy creations that Ruth could find. Her clothes were high street. Her knickers were the pure, unadulterated luxury of a designer brand.

When KJ had the baby, Ruth had twenty eight nappy squares sewn in white silk. She presented them to the new mother wrapped in coconut leaves.

"You're a crazy lady," Kesia said. "Baby poo needs towelling."

"My niece deserves silk," Ruth replied.

To this day, that child receives seven pairs of silk knickers by post, every year on her birthday, from her anonymous sponsor, together with a big parcel of books.

And please don't ask me to divulge how a mere book acquired such intelligence. My sources must remain anonymous to protect them. Just remember that a book has many layers. Jungle drums and Chinese whispers are more than letters standing side by side.

My sources told me that Ruth purchased three copies at the launch. (I approve wholeheartedly of abundant spending so Ruth got my silent cheer.)

One copy of *An Appetite for Words,* signed by KJ, was to go to the child who will be sixteen all too soon. One copy Ruth kept for herself. She didn't need Kesia's autograph in it. The book was hers to keep, a link to their shared history and memory. Books and words were a sanitised way to resolve the past and shape the future. Ruth was undecided on the fate of the third copy.

"Should I send it to that brother of mine?" she mused.

Hell's bells sweetheart, from what I know of the man, he isn't worth the postage.

By the time Sajud revealed his unholy mess to his sister and asked for her help, Kesia had a bump that could not be misinterpreted. Ruth and KJ had skirted each other at first meeting, curious, intimidated, defensive and more than a little competitive for his attentions.

"A baby," Ruth said, "how completely miraculous."

I wondered if Sajud the seducer had tried to sell another Immaculate Conception story. Or opt for a version of the second coming?

Ruth had so many questions.

"Where would they live – Africa or Britain? What kind of name would they choose – black or white? Could she be godmother and aunt? Was Kesia a Catholic? How many bridesmaids did she plan to have?"

"Won't the bishop be surprised?" asked KJ.

And then – the stonker – Sajud announced that ordination was still his goal.

"Isn't there a sin or two involved?"

"Absolution comes through confession," he had replied to Ruth as he walked out.

Six months later, after the benefit of silent contemplation in a monastery up a mountain in the Italian Alps, Sajud took holy orders. It was final. God had triumphed over an earthly kingdom.

Two months after her brother's desertion, Ruth found an answer to one of her questions. She was godmother, aunt, collaborator and pariah. She welcomed Kesia's little surprise into the world of a convent. Kesia nursed her baby girl for two weeks before the nuns forced the next steps. The child was sent to The Gambia. Missionaries would arrange the details.

"But the father is from Sierra Leone," Ruth argued.

The nuns nodded politely. Africa was Africa.

"Black babies needed proper roots, no matter where God chose to plant a tree," they said.

I figured those nuns might think they knew a lot about God. But they didn't have a good grip on cultural geography. The Gambia was ninety percent Muslim. God and that girl child were sure to be confused.

The books called it Post-natal Depression. Kesia refused to eat or speak. The doctors suggested her condition was temporary. Drugs were the answer. The baby might have gone, her breast milk may have dried, but the smell of soft flesh lingered in Kesia's nostrils. Ruth understood the stench of reality and took control. She cooked comfort food, her famous coconut soup. Kesia began to eat a little.

Ruth borrowed videos of old films. The women sat in silence and watched other worlds. Kesia became fixated by *The Godfather*. 'You can never lose your family, never', was her favourite line.

Ruth thought 'Revenge is a dish that tastes best when it is cold' was more inspirational.

Though Kesia stumbled through the months half-awake, Ruth slept easily. She believed her choice to be a good one. It might have been different. But it wasn't. In their case it was the only option for two single women, and best for the baby.

Fifteen years later at the book signing of *An Appetite for Words*, Ruth stood towards the back of the queue. Three copies, a signature requested, would Kesia acknowledge or refuse? Neither as it turned out. Their eyes met. My KJ said nothing.

"Would you like a dedication?" asked the sales assistant.

"No thank you, a signature is fine," replied Ruth.

KJ signed me, her precious first edition, and offered up my virginity. Ruth scooped my bulk into her tote, collected the two other copies and turned to leave. Kesia continued with the next in line.

It wasn't how I dreamed we would part… my turn for a nasty surprise.

As Ruth reached the door, she felt a tap on her left shoulder and turned. The sales assistant proffered a small piece of folded paper. Ruth took it. Inside was a telephone number. She put the note in her coat pocket, left the building and caught the number 63 bus back to her flat. It was only when she retired to her bed to start reading her copy that she noticed she had lost one of the books.

So I sat on a table beside the bed of a woman whose story I thought I knew. Another week brought more surprises. I learned that Ruth had followed her niece's adoption trail, by means undisclosed and clearly devious. Over time Ruth had extended her role to include being an anonymous sponsor to a child called Amani. Accepted, adored and safe from girlhood surprises, Amani blossomed into a feisty and well educated young woman whose future held untold advantages. The child's name meant peace. Would the journey of the book belie the reputation of its recipient?

A month later Ruth made two telephone calls. The first was long distance. The African connection crackled but I could hear his voice clearly.

"Your identity is safe. She didn't betray you," said Ruth.

A sigh of relief, a discussion about the book's content and a final remark.

"Bit cheeky," Sajud said to his sister, "Kesia including your recipe for Spicy Coconut Soup. That's our cultural heritage."

"I took it as her way of saying thanks – to me, a friend indeed and all that," Ruth replied.

"I shall say a prayer and give thanks to God."

"You must read Kesia's thoughts on religion. Try page 89."

"She was always good with words."

On the fourth ring of Ruth's second call, KJ answered. A date, a time and a venue were arranged. Afterwards Ruth walked to the post office with her copy of the book. It was addressed to a teenager in The Gambia.

I imagined her brother in his vestments bowed before an ornate cross in his African cathedral. Heaven or Hell, saint or sinner, Sajud or Judas – whatever the anagram, wherever the place, Sajud was a habitual game player. I knew that preaching in church wouldn't make him honourable any more than living in a garage would make me a car!

From *An Appetite for Words* by Kesia Jaskins: page 89:

> *For as long as I can remember, the love of God was always a bit of a laugh in our family. My mother was agnostic, my father a lapsed Methodist who embraced alcohol with all the zeal of a late developer making up for lost time. I never really got God or booze. From observation, both paths seemed to promise more pain than pleasure in what they delivered.*
>
> *My mother had a cousin who was a devout Roman Catholic. The family considered the cousin deluded when they felt charitable, deranged when they did not. My father's regular demand, after a glass or few of wine, was to ask how he knew that Adam and Eve were Catholics. The answer was always a variation on who else would be alone in a garden with a naked woman and be tempted by a piece of fruit? I didn't really find his joke very amusing but the family grinned and tut-tutted over his attempts to hold centre stage.*

And what could I do but smile when people with measurable IQs agreed that Mary was still a virgin after giving birth to a son whose father was an invisible man from outer space? And that a man called Pope, who wore a party hat and a long white dress for serious formal occasions, was infallible?

Of course comedy comes in many guises. Some of that religious cant qualifies as black humour in my mind. And the more politically incorrect the jokes are, the louder I'm likely to guffaw. I'm not specifically anti-Christian. I can smile at jokes about any denomination – Muslim, Hindu, Buddhist, Jewish and everything in between. I think comedy can do what religion only purports to offer. People who laugh together share a bond of affirmation. What makes you feel more uplifted – a story about a man being tortured on a cross and betrayed by his friends, or a joke about miracles? You choose.

Judas laughed out loud when I told him the joke about four Catholic ladies at a tea party, bragging about their sons. One woman said that her son was a priest and when he entered a room, everyone called him Father. Another chirped that her son had made bishop and earned the title Your Grace. Not to be outdone, the third mother announced that her progeny was now a cardinal and smugly shared that he is addressed as Your Eminence. The fourth member of the group drank her tea in silence and ate a cake or two before quipping, "My son is a tall, dark, handsome body-builder. When he walks into a room, people say, "Oh my god..."

170

Judas thought it best not to share the joke with the cardinal until after he was ordained.

I never found a joke about a priest who got his lover pregnant and then abandoned mother and child. Is there one? Answers on a postcard please.

Something Spicy – Coconut Soup

4 spring onions, finely chopped
2 tablespoons nut oil
3 tablespoons mild curry paste
2 teaspoons ginger, grated
1 teaspoon lemon grass, finely chopped
I kg spinach
600ml coconut milk
600ml vegetable stock
Sea salt and freshly ground pepper
1 teaspoon lime juice

1. Gently fry the spring onions in the oil with the curry paste, ginger and lemon grass.
2. Add spinach and sauté until wilted.
3. Pour in the coconut milk, stock and bring to the boil
4. Transfer the mixture to a blender.
5. Puree in batches until smooth
6. Stir in the lime juice
7. Decorate with a swirl of coconut milk

Serves 6

Something Savoury

A hedgehog might be cute. But would you want to cuddle it? Or feed it and take it home? So I pondered as Judy James clutched me tightly and peered into the mirror of the staff toilet at the bus depot. Her tuft of blond spikes was a tribute to cheap gel and dexterous fingers.

"Frigging heck," she spat at the mirror. "He won't even stop for a drink."

It was an hour until her shift was over, quiet time. Tidy up and plan her escape. Clock watch till lock up and walk out. Her office was open from 9 a.m. until 5 p.m., Monday to Friday. There was usually a queue when it opened. Umbrellas were the most popular request. According to her boss, aka The Oracle, over three thousand umbrellas found their way to the lost property depot each year. Only a few were ever claimed. Between Christmas and New Year the office packed up all the orphans and sent them to a charity which sold them in shops, staffed by volunteers, around the country.

I was quite fascinated where they sent the weird bits and bobs. Who bought abandoned breast implants (three sets found on three different buses during one month), or a giraffe skull? Wacky or what? I figured she should write a book about it.

"And your story madam?" Judy asked a lurid pink, folding umbrella. "Who left you on the number 47 bus?"

Books outnumbered umbrellas by ten to one but I was the only signed copy of the title, *An Appetite for Words*. There were lots of other items that had absconded from their owners. How could someone forget to take a lawnmower off a bus? Mind you Judy seemed more impressed that someone had managed to persuade a driver to have it on the bus. Though not all lost items were found, like the misplaced Rolex worth £40,000. The staff award for Lost of the Year went to a speech therapist. She reclaimed a suitcase of battery-powered vibrators. Used them in children's mouths to stimulate tongue movement! Or so she said, blushing. I didn't want to think about it... too gross.

The lost, the forgotten and the discarded items were delivered daily – more umbrellas in winter, fewer books in summer. Judy didn't mind sorting the debris. She worked on her own. Nobody bothered her. She wore her headphones and listened to whatever music she fancied. It was a big bonus not having to talk to anyone but herself.

The sorting office used to be open half day on Saturday until re-organisation was announced. That signalled staff cuts. Judy liked working Saturdays. She didn't get paid extra but the other half of the day was given off in lieu. Something to do with anti-social hours.

"Stuff the toss," she told her fellow workers, "it doesn't really matter to me."

But it did. Saturday might be mad with enquires but at least it was four hours instead of eight.

"B-b-b-bummer really," she had said to The Oracle when the new schedules were announced.

"Does you good," The Oracle replied. "Hiding yourself away from the public won't cure your defect."

I was shocked. Is that what they teach staff these days on the human resources course?

"Stutters and stammers never killed anyone," Judy's mother said whenever she confessed tales of torture from her peers at school. If only!

Judy knew the science, had read the blurb, endured hours of speech therapy, suffered the consequences and their lack of results.

"No physical impediment or malformation," declared the medical fraternity.

"She'll grow out it," was the accepted wisdom. "Five percent of young children suffer with stuttering. The majority develop enough confidence to overcome the problem by adolescence."

Duhhhh – so how do you develop confidence amongst chums with fluid plosives?

Judy subscribed to booze and nu-rave... got pissed, spoke straight, looked dumb and scary or knew the visual language and stood proud and clever. She wore designer hoodies, bowler hats borrowed from images in *Clockwork Orange*, gender-fuck suits and thunder-thigh pants, cleavage suggested but suppressed.

"A wardrobe with attitude," Judy said.

"You ever considered heels?" asked The Oracle.

Yeah up your b-b-b-butt, she thought.

"Heels are to women like t-t-ties are to g-g-guys," she replied. The Oracle shook his head and stopped commenting on how to bed a bloke.

"Some women just can't be helped," he said.

"That-t-t what-t-t your manual on team building suggests? Like you ever wear a tie, unless a management meeting at central office is on the horizon," she replied.

When Judy met Hjalmar, he was off his face with vodka shots. He told her she glimmered like the Northern Lights. High on tequila twists, she woke up in his bed on a Sunday morning feeling more submerged mollusc than twinkling aurora. A few parties later, lots of noise and plenty of boozy action, Judy dreaded Friday the thirteenth as much as desired it. Hjalmar had suggested a date. Like a proper date, drinks, talking, maybe dinner... just the two of them... at a wine bar. She knew he did something with computers, had grown up in Sweden, read books in different languages and danced like a crazy spider. Hjalmar could move nonstop for an hour on a dance floor, legs, arms, head flung around with ecstatic fervour.

First rule on how not to stutter was: AVOID ANXIETY.

No pressure then, Judy just had to stay sober, smile with stuck-on self-esteem and forget her nickname: Fridge Magnet. She had earned that tag when she started in lost property. It saluted her Goth metal period. Geisha white make-up, black lipstick, T-shirts with crude, provocative slogans and metal piercings with dingles and dangles attached through every surface and orifice she could use. Even The Oracle had given a good impression of respect for the first week.

The stutter blew her street cred out of the depot.

Friday the thirteenth's motto was be prepared, even though she'd got kicked out of Girl Guides for refusing to participate appropriately in team building events. Ever tried being a team member where your colleagues give you a list of instructions to read out loud with every order beginning with a plosive?

"B-b-b-boil some water."

"T-t-t-take these."

"D-d-d-dig a trench."

"G-g-g-go now."

And a double douzy, triple squared, with "G-g-go g-g-get t-t-two -b-b-boxes of d-d-d-iced t-t-t-urnips."

When one of the team asked her to repeat that instruction, Judy got "fuck off" out without a hitch. End of that association and beginning of solitary pursuits. However for the Hjalmar rendezvous she planned to arrive with a prepared list of topics that she felt comfortable discussing – food and literature – all starting with sibilants or fricatives.

I was her bonus knight in matt paper. *An Appetite for Words*, travelled without a ticket, on bus route 63, signed by the author, Kesia Jaskins, rescued from the pile of lost libraries. Perfect – words, writer and reader, all three rolled off her tongue. The sweet potato recipe in the book was the best kick-arse reminder that she had discovered.

Second rule on how not to stutter was: RELAX.

Hjalmar was ensconced at the bar when she arrived, carrying me in her bag. Quick decision needed – pretend she hadn't seen him and head for the loo to fine tune any travel damage to her hair and makeup? Or play it cool, half smile, wrist-flick hello and saunter to the adjacent stool.

Breathing deeply, my girl Judy opted for the latter. Preliminaries over, drinks ordered, he suggested they moved to an alcove, a sofa with squashy cushions that spoke volumes. Whenever she moved the air in the cushion went pshhhhh. Now was that an omen or what?

Shhh was definitely a sibilant. The gods were on her side.

Hjalmar wasn't big on the small talk. Judy relaxed even more. I guessed they were both nervous. She noticed the tiny spasms, a foot jerk here, a twitchy hand there. Was that gratitude or misplaced maternal as a hot flush flooded through her body? Fingers and pages crossed. She didn't blush. It would so ruin her face paint.

Hjalmar talked about his work in computer programming. I didn't understand a single thing but Judy found it easy to listen and smile. She didn't have to say much. The occasional, "really" did the trick. Upward inflection to make it a question – really? Flat, downward slide of the voice to suggest interest and solicit further information. Really, exclamation mark, indicated excitement and discovery. Well done Judy! The background music and ambient noise was good enough to hide her stumble on b-buses as she tried to make her job sound more exciting than it was.

"You should write a TV series," he said. "You must have a laugh about what's lost and found."

Hey boyo, I wanted to scream, be careful who you insult. This abandoned copy of *An Appetite for Words* is on your side.

"You want to hear my vibrators in a suitcase story?" she asked.

He responded with a sort of emission that sounded like a pantomime guffaw.

And that's when I saw it happen.

Hjalmar the Swedish sex bomb morphed into Hyde the head case. His left arm jerked from his side to his shoulder and flopped. His head flipped from centre front to right shoulder. His eyes blinked like deranged traffic lights. Out of order, out of order!

Was this a practical joke?

"I don't find this very funny at all," she whispered to him. The spasms continued. Other people stared at them. She sank further into the sofa.

"C-c-can you c-c-cut the c-c-rap," she asked.

The antics ceased abruptly. She hung her head, tears threatening to spill. Her secret was unlocked.

Third rule on how not to stutter was: FOCUS ON THE EXTERNAL.

A waitress wearing the name badge, Lauren, came to their alcove.

"You guys okay?"

Hjalmar and Judy nodded in silence.

"Want to order the same again?"

"Yes," they replied in unison.

Lauren raised her eyebrows and departed.

"You don't have to stay," he said. "You've stuck around longer than most."

"Sorry," she replied, "I'm not used to public performances. It's a lot quieter where I hang out."

Neither spoke. The waitress returned with the drinks. Nervous but not thirsty they gulped them down in one. I wondered if he was being polite or had just chosen to ignore her verbal gash. Better to get it out in the open and end the date now. It could be another disaster to file under her memories.

"Look it's really kind of you," she said, "but there's nothing I can do about it. I've tried."

"What are you talking about?" he asked.

"I stammered back there."

"When? During the first part or the finale of my exhibition?"

"It's okay. I guess I just like to blend in with the cushions. Don't really know how to do street theatre. Comes with being the class freak," she admitted.

"Skitsnygg!"

What sort of a word is that? Not between my covers, that's for certain.

Judy look perplexed. He explained it was Swedish for fucking marvellous.

Well that's a new one for a book I thought.

She bit on her lower lip, said nothing, breathed.

"Tourette's Syndrome," he confided. "I get tics and uncontrollable movements."

"How come?"

"Born that way. It's full on when I get nervous."

"You nervous with me?"

"Fuck, yes."

"We're just having a d-d-drink."

"You're gorgeous."

"You're a spunk yourself."

"Why not?"

It was her turn to confess. The speech impediment. They both sighed and smiled. Secrets traded.

"Freaky Friday or what?" he asked. "Let's cut the crap, have dinner and spend the weekend shagging?"

"Sounds normal to me," she agreed. "Can I read you something from a book I found in lost property?"

That was my cue. *An Appetite for Words* was centre stage.

"Go for it. Want to hold my hand?" he replied.

"That seems a bit main stream romantic," she said.

"Nah, keep me bits anchored. Not a great start to seduction if I get wildly turned on and smack you in the ear hole."

I shuddered as I reflected that their version of sex was definitely going to have its impact moments.

Judy smiled, grabbed his hand and opened my covers to read.

From An Appetite for Words: page 103:

Fun and games, that's what the newspapers say. Love is all about fun and games. I kept the photographs of some of those fun times: Judas and I picnicking in the Yorkshire Dales, skiing in Switzerland, cycling in Portugal, partying in London. There were other images like Judas, his sister and I huddling, pebble punctured, on Brighton beach, frozen, munching soggy fish and chips as the grey sky drizzled gloom on a chill summer day. But not even God, commanding all his force majeure, could dampen our fun.

And the games we played to tease and please each other. Judas liked music. He loved to introduce me to something new, something that challenged Western notions of the great and the good. We listened to singers from Senegal to Samoa, danced to rhythms that inspired movement, applauded sounds from instruments that had no listing in a dictionary. It was uplifting and seductive to be part of discovering a new world of sound. Judas also loved sweet potatoes, cooked any way I chose to experiment, food to savour.

My favourite game was finders-feelers. In those days I wrote appalling bad doggerel and left a chain of them as an obstacle course for Judas to follow.

'To find where it's at, look under a hard hat' meant the next clue was under the toilet seat lid.

By the time my devoted Sherlock had collected pointers from letter boxes to coal holes he was delighted to arrive at my endgame. His very favourite rendezvous was me lying naked in a bath filled with scented bubbles, plastic ducks that glowed in the dark, a bottle of fizzy wine, one glass, two strawberries. Adam and Eve might have done it first but I upgraded their style.

But publications have another section. The agony aunt, the letters which detail the games that went wrong, the words that described what was so not fun. The column space devoted to the other person, the third party in a relationship, was not the stuff of punch lines. Lies, betrayal and grief don't raise much of a laugh. Especially when you're the victim. Did God laugh at me, at my naivety? He certainly smiled on Judas. His black-eyed boy made it to cardinal.

I just wanted to be normal, to fit in, to have

what others had, so people around me would tick the she's-okay box. It's a safe form of invisibility because although we might pretend that we would like to stand out and be noticed, most of us wouldn't opt for freak-in-a-cage status in a zoo with twenty four access.

Holding my new born daughter made me feel normal but special, a queen with her princess in a hospital ward of parents that would fit in to any story in every town. Giving my child up for adoption and returning as a reconstituted single woman to my old world might have seemed normal. I might have looked like the neighbours. But the damaged freak caged in my lactating body screamed otherwise.

P.S. So what's normal? A book's a book whether it's fiction, self-help or a pile of poetry. If my girls had focused more on what makes them content then we'd have all ended up normal.

Something Savoury – Sweet Potato Cakes with Savoury Salsa Topping

425g mashed sweet potato
1 egg, beaten
1 onion, chopped
1 tablespoon coriander, chopped
1 tablespoon chutney
½ teaspoon ground ginger
Salt, pepper
2 tablespoons vegetable oil

1. Mix egg, onion, coriander, chutney, ginger, salt and pepper with the mashed sweet potato.
2. Scoop and mould into palm-sized circles about 2cm thick, then chill for 30 minutes and make the topping.
3. Heat the oil in a frying pan and fry the chilled potato cakes for 2-3 minutes each side until crisp and lightly browned.

Savoury Topping

1 avocado, flesh chopped
4 tomatoes, chopped
2 sticks celery, chopped
1 lime, juiced
1 lemon, juiced
Handful of parsley, chopped

1. Mix all ingredients.
2. Serve with hot sweet potato cakes.

Serves 4

Something Sharp

Home is a contentious word for a book. Does it mean where you were conceived? In that case, home is where you sit beside your author. Sometimes it's scribblings in a notebook. Other times it's a draft on a computer. Best times are hard copy, sitting on a desk, waiting patiently for your author to trawl the lines, red pen poised, final polish charge. You know your maker's thoughts, get good at guessing their directions and squirm at some of their edits.

I want to challenge. Why leave that detail out? How can you expect someone to read between those lines? How many drafts are you planning? It's difficult to live through the process although I know it's all part of the ignominies we manuscripts have to endure in the comfort of our home. Adoration, angst, writer's block and the odd tantrum are part of our maturation. By graduation we're a printed book with prospects of a new abode.

For some books, that might be one careful owner, a lifetime on a shelf with crossword games, Thesaurus, the Bible, and some historical tome parked beside you. My aspiration was to be the copy KJ kept. I fancied that I would nestle conspicuously on the shelf in her living room amongst all the previous first editions. I imagined we could vie for honours. Which of us had sold the most copies? Collected the most prestigious award? I believed I would be in with a chance, the latest, the best acclaimed, the most widely translated.

KJ had other plans. Clearly my destiny was for me to be her special envoy. She recognised that I would be the one that got out there, saw the world, experienced real life readers. I was printed to be part of the circulation and not a museum piece.

So I got excited when Ruth took me. Like ending up with the good fairy at the end of KJ''s nightmare, I told the other copies. When Ruth left me on a bus it seemed a very careless approach to moving house. Reading about the homeless is one thing but who really wants to go there?

Home with Judy, of hedgehog head fame, was one of those interludes I recall, in hindsight, with more pleasure than the experience itself. Being privy to the details of KJ's tortured love life I didn't fancy shacking up with two youngsters exploring therapeutic sex.

So when I landed in Lauren's life I was optimistic. More mature female, established relationship, I imagined order and comfort. If only!

"Tragic," moaned the twenty-seven year old manager at the wine bar where Lauren worked.

In retrospect it was the perfect summary of a sordid episode that nearly pulped my pages.

"Middle age… it's just tragic how middle aged women are invisible," the manager repeated.

"Speak for yourself," said Lauren. "Pete focuses on me late, early, on time, whenever, whatever."

"I'm not middle-aged yet, you cheeky cow. Look at that one," the manager nodded towards a thirtyish, lone female, perched at the bar, sipping Beaujolais Nouveau whilst texting. "Bet she's doing a bogus progress report on her fun night out. Tragic!"

"Or she's waiting for her lesbian lover who's CEO of the largest hedge fund on the planet."

"Yeah and Prince Harry's going to whisk me away to Mexico any time soon," laughed the manager.

"Now that would be tragic," replied Lauren.

"So what rattles you?"

"Tragic is more mundane in my life – a mobile phone with no credit, laddered tights five minutes before this shift started, no milk in the fridge for Pete's coffee first thing in the morning," Lauren replied.

185

"Beyond tragic," sighed the manager, "that's epic. You need to get a life. One that's got some breathe in it."

On Friday the thirteenth Lauren's shift had been busy but not frantic. When she started at 15:00 the yummy mummy brigade was finishing their coffee and cake amidst flashes of nipple, and an engorged breast or two. Then those infant-feeding women packed their body bits into Boden and stuffed their babies into the latest ergonomic push chairs. Pilates-erect, juggling designer bags and organic shopping they trundled off, sugar charged, to collect their little poppets from prep school.

"Tragic," the manager warned again. "Never going there. Why sign up for sagging tits?"

Friday nights were unpredictable but precisely timed. At 17:13 the place was empty. At 17:15 it was action stations with office workers, finished for the week, flowing through the doors. Happy hour ready, credit card primed. Corks popped as promotions were celebrated, redundancies drowned and romances launched. By 19:00 the theatre going crowd had departed and the diners settled for gourmet food and yet more bottles of whatever they fancied and could afford. The remainder of the shift flew by as the dedicated drinkers and diners rallied for lust, while pining for love.

"Weirdoes or what?" whispered the manager to Lauren, indicating a couple half-snuggled on a sofa in the low lit alcove.

"New to me, you ever seen them before?"

The manager shook her head, "You get first guess."

"Not poseur piss heads. They're drinking beer, the cheapest on the list."

Lauren and her manager liked to categorise customers into tribes. The poseur-piss-heads were young, single, prosperous and out to impress. Consensus was the bigger the cocktail, the smaller the office space. Then there were the when-we-lot, turning thirty and desperate to promote an aura of lived-in gaiety from an imagined past.

"When we were in Ibiza the club was heaving with X Factor judges. Did you know that I shagged that…?"

The when-we lot poisoned themselves with champagne, branded if flush, house label if mortgaged.

The final category was the constrained-by-circumstances group. They were those grateful to be back in the game – the dumped, the divorced and the social networking demoted. They ordered house chardonnay and merlot.

These three tribes made up the bulk of the bar's customers but Lauren loved to find an outsider, someone who didn't quite conform, and assign them a new label. So Judy, lost and found wage slave from the bus depot, got labelled Banshee Babe and her date, the Spastic Stud.

"Keep your voice down," warned Lauren. "You'll get us arrested for that."

"Political correctness is a load of shite. Those two are weird, end of."

"What's wrong with a prickle head, killer kohl eyes and biker boots that could crack a street light?" smiled Lauren.

"The friend's kind of cute," agreed the manager. "Like his blond locks and nervous twitch."

"Not going all romantic on me are you?" asked Lauren.

Her manager was still young enough to sneer about love over a beer or a bottle of house wine. Lauren dreamt of heroes. She could spot a moody Heathcliff (he who brooded and glowered when his prize noticed other men); a shy Mr Darcy (short, chatty females who touched his tie were a give-away) or an X factor (beer and burger boy with a try-hard T-shirt).

The banter stopped and the opinion got revised with the two customers performed a full scale exhibition. The

187

manager freaked at their outburst. Lauren walked over to the alcove and tried her charm.

"Celebrating Friday the thirteenth?" she asked them.

"Ja, it's Scandinavian," the blond lad muttered.

Lauren raised her eyebrows. "Mmm you've certainly caught the attention of everyone. But could I ask you to keep it down? This is more a mood and mulch sort of place. Our regulars can only take a little of the public performance approach. That okay?"

"Paraskevidekatriaphobia," he toasted.

"What's that mean?" said Lauren.

"Fear of the date," he replied as his girlfriend gazed in adoration. "It comes from the Norse goddess called Frigga and the amalgamation of the Greek for number thirteen."

"Well I didn't know that," admitted Lauren.

I didn't either so I awarded him a gold star for book learning. But I wasn't convinced that he was any more than a smart-arse.

"Would you like to order more drinks?" asked Lauren.

They shook their heads and left quietly.

"Date over?" asked the manager.

"I think he's got some sort of condition," said Lauren. "I reckon it'll be a Mills and Boon ending."

"Home for a bonk then," sneered the manager.

I reckoned there was no way of knowing. It was safe to suggest that they'd never return, whatever the scenario.

"Oh look what I've scored," said Lauren, scooping me up from the sofa. "It's Kesia Jaskins' new book. Something to read on the bus home."

So endeth my role as the silent souvenir that played gooseberry to young love. Bonus was that I got to travel in Lauren's faux leather, mock designer bag with satin lining. Step up from the rough canvas of Judy's satchel.

Lauren turned out to be what I call an indiscriminate

reader. Skimmed the words, not much reflection, average recall. It took her three weeks to read me cover to cover.

"Might try one of these recipes," she said to the manager.

"Wouldn't think they'd be your Pete's taste."

Now that was a hyperbole. Her Pete was a junk food addict.

"You'd be surprised by what Pete likes," replied Lauren.

The look on the manager's face suggested otherwise.

"You going to tell him tonight then?"

"He'll probably be asleep. I just want a good book, a hot bath and a warm bed... bliss."

Only her Pete wasn't asleep when she walked through the door with me in her hands. He was wide awake, upright and rigid, almost frothing at the mouth.

"Where have you been?" he asked in a low monotone. Lauren explained... four times... the vagaries of public transport and bus timetables.

I did wonder if he was deaf.

"Why didn't you call?"

"No credit on my phone. Forgot to top up. I am so, so sorry, really, really sorry."

I wondered why she felt the need for grovelling. Surely an apology was enough.

"Who were you with?"

"Apart from a hundred customers?" she joked.

Silence.

I could smell the tension. Fear is rancid.

The first half of their familiar game kicked off.

"I love you," she screamed.

"You're my woman," he shouted. Whack!

From their first slogging match that occurred when I went to stay with her I learned the history. After ten years of marriage to a mild-mannered accountant, safe as soap and bland to match, Lauren had walked out. Bubble wrapped had meant long slow suffocation.

"A life half-lived is no life," she said.

Had she found it exhilarating at first? Did Pete embody her notions of passion, spontaneity and risk?

Over the next weeks I learnt about her life with Pete. Like the time she was late home. Pete had shredded her underwear before she returned to their flat.

"I lost my mobile."

"Liar!"

"Make-up sex is brilliant," he said.

She wore a long sleeved shirt to cover the bruises. Then there was the passionate tussle against the coat rack.

"Bus didn't turn up."

"Bitch!"

Her doctor did not ask outright. He confirmed her wrist was sprained, not broken.

"Stupid me," she said to her manager, "I bumped into the oven."

"Clumsy is to cruel as kindness is to kill," said her wine bar manager.

"Look he made me this card. It's got real flowers and a hand written poem. He's sorry and I love him. We were just having a rough patch."

"Broken ribs are more than a hiccough."

Pete phoned two or three times a shift.

"He's just a romantic," Lauren sighed.

"He's obsessed," said her manager.

"He loves me," she confided to explain a bandaged arm. "It's just a little cut."

"The fucker slashed your paintings," the manager said.

"He thought I was going to leave."

"He's a nutter."

"He's sometimes high maintenance," Lauren agreed.

"You know what happens when you overwater a pot plant?" her manager asked.

I was worried about my own safety when he burnt her entire collection of historical romance novels – two hundred books from *Tale of Two Cities* to *Gone with the Wind* – for a staff celebration that went on too long. Thankfully, Lauren kept me in her bag. Everywhere Lauren went, that bag got to go. I was so glad to be invisible.

Unlike the blue line on the pregnancy test which was not.

"Tragic," said the manager.

"I'm forty-two and I just know Pete will be delighted."

The manager burst into tears, "He won't change you know. What are you going to do when he tosses your baby against a wall?"

"The baby will help our relationship."

"Give me your mobile. I'm putting my personal number on speed dial," insisted her manager. "It's listed under ICE."

"What?"

"In case of emergency."

"You just don't know my Pete."

Lauren left it there to appease her.

Pete listened to the news. A dependent screaming for Lauren's attention and body, twenty-four seven for years to come. Pete knew Lauren well, every part of her body. He knew that if he punched her just below her left breast, she crumpled. A kick to her right buttock and she rolled onto her side. That night the familiar morphed into a new game plan.

"Help me," Lauren cried into the phone.

Her manager dialled the police and said a prayer.

Was heaven on holiday when Lauren threw me into the circus ring?

Later, kneeling on the floor, rocking, arms wrapped around her abdomen, Lauren gulped air as tears dripped silently onto my blood splattered pages.

"Never would have picked her as a violent type. You think she's being drinking?" asked the police officer.

"God only knows, these days the women are as bad as the men," replied the detective in charge of the crime scene. "Here's the culprit," he said, pointing at me.

I lay there, open at page 169, stinking of Pete's venom and Lauren's defence. Hot and sour, my words stared up at the beholder.

"If only these pages could talk, hey?" said the policeman.

Read me like an open book I screamed silently.

Relegated to a piece of evidence, I was flung into a clear plastic bag, and packaged for the prosecution.

It was tragic all right.

From An Appetite for Words: page 169:

> *Being in love is about extremes, the best, the worst, pain, passion, a moment, forever.... a bit like sweet and sour. Or in my case hot and sour. I was never sweet on someone. I'm not that type of person. I either fancied them or I didn't. No blow hot, blow cold. No maybe, no tepid to tingle. Just definitely yes, or decidedly no. When a relationship was on the boil I bubbled. When it was over I cooled rapidly. Frisson to frigid. I didn't do scenes or angst. Walking out was sign enough. That way things didn't turn sour or putrid, no remonstrations or sulky silences; closure was swift, clean and final.*

Just watch a chef cleaver a carrot from its pretty but defunct top in preparation for the cooking. Being in love is an ingredient but not the final dish.

In China a well prepared dish is expected to appeal to all senses. Its taste must enchant the tongue, its colours flirt with the eye and its aroma seduce. The sound of satisfied diners indicates pleasure and purpose are balanced. The extremes of texture and taste, the crisp and the smooth, the subtle and the spiced are brought together. The ying and the yang, each separate, opposite but inter-connected.

That's how it was with Judas. Black and white, male and female, spiritual and profane, giver and taker, performer and watcher.

I thought I knew the difference between being in love versus loving. Too often I had looked only at the aesthetics of what was served up. An athletic body, a sense of humour, a fast car can be dazzling. I forgot to check the ingredients. Too often the surface hid the flaws that undermined the substance of a person. Capricious experiences made me cautious. I vowed to be more discerning, to choose more wisely.

I changed course. Listening was more seductive than looking. Ugly heroes like Cyrano de Bergerac and John Wilkes knew that opportunity came with words that flattered and cosseted. I was blinded by Judas-beauty, brawn and brains – a perfect combination.

Childbirth is the ultimate love-in. I thought I would die from the pain. I fell in love when my baby was delivered. I loved my daughter enough to give her away. It was a hot, sweet and sour experience.

But it was never balanced.
That's when I knew for certain that men saw
it differently. Judas was right. His God was male.
God had to be a man because only a man would
sacrifice his child.
A woman would kill herself first.

P.S. What do you want me to say? I am an object who became the subject with no interference from an editor. KJ gave me life as a book. Lauren used me as a weapon to launch Pete's after-life.

Something Sharp – Hot and Sour Soup

150g chicken, shredded
Marinade:
      1 teaspoon soy sauce
      ½ teaspoon sesame oil
      1 teaspoon cornflour
60g tofu / bean curd, cut into small squares
4 Chinese mushrooms, sliced
200g bamboo shoots, finely sliced into thin strips
2 tablespoons assorted mushrooms, sliced
200g frozen or fresh peas
1500ml water
3 vegetable stock cubes
1 teaspoon granulated sugar
1½ tablespoons soy sauce
1 tablespoon sherry
2 tablespoons red rice vinegar or red wine vinegar
1 teaspoon sesame oil
1 tablespoon cornflour dissolved in 50ml water
1 egg, beaten
1 spring onion, finely chopped
Salt to taste
White pepper to taste

1. Mix marinade ingredients and marinate shredded chicken for 30 minutes.
2. In a saucepan bring the water and stock cubes to the boil.

3. Add the bamboo shoots, mushrooms, and the peas. Stir.
4. Add the tofu / bean curd.
5. Bring back to a boil and add the marinated chicken.
6. Stir in the sugar, soy sauce, sherry, vinegar and sesame oil.
7. Test the soup and add salt and pepper to adjust the taste if desired.
8. Mix the cornflour and water.
9. Lower the heat.
10. Slowly pour the cornflour mixture into the soup, stirring as it is added, until thickened.
11. Return the soup to the boil and then remove the saucepan from the stove.
12. Slowly drop in the beaten egg, stirring in one direction at the same time.
13. Add the spring onion.
14. Serve hot.

Serves 4

Something Shared

I owe my renaissance to an unlikely heroine, the sensibly shod, fragrant Francis, charity shop volunteer. Languishing in the apartheid of donations, I balanced on a stool in the back of the shop, between a box marked To Be Sorted and two plastic sacks leaking eau de damp shoes. My title, *An Appetite for Words,* was clearly visible although KJ's name was hidden by something that resembled a Rorschach test. Splattered with blotches and speckles, smelling dank from too long in that plastic evidence bag, it was a friendless existence.

You might think me ungrateful. Some ignorant whippersnapper who had forgotten lessons learned in evidence processing. Me – consigned to the archives forever more. Survival had its price.

I might have been marooned there for months if Francis hadn't arrived so early for her Thursday morning shift. She was one of my favourites, really relished decent literature. No airport best sellers for her. She had a vocabulary that flagged a first rate education. She would complete the *Guardian* crossword in fifteen minutes without a dictionary.

With the other volunteer yet to arrive, and no customers rifling through the merchandise, Francis knew she had time for a cuppa and perhaps ten minutes for reading. When she picked me up, carried me into the kitchen and announced loudly to the room, "Definitely option one, DO IT NOW," I knew my fortunes were about to change.

The kitchen was Spartan – a kettle, a two-ringed hot plate and an under-counter refrigerator unplugged from the electricity supply.

"Black tea then," Francis muttered as she viewed the opened carton of milk with suspicion.

She chose a blue, willow patterned, china cup and saucer from the collection of crockery. Souvenirs from a sort-through-the donations which some volunteer had not been able to part with. Francis liked to drink tea from a cup and saucer.

"Nobody bothers these days," she once told a volunteer. "It's mugs or cardboard cups, drink in or take out."

The oncology unit had left her with a distaste for both.

She poured the boiling water in the yellow teapot with a cracked spout. A hand-made poster was blue-tacked to the wall. There were four instructions on it:

> DO IT NOW (if you can)
> DELAY (if you're not sure)
> DELEGATE (if you can't)
> DUMP (if it's not saleable)

All that a volunteer shop assistant in a retail charity outlet needed to know.

I reckoned Francis was more a DO IT NOW and a DUMP kind of worker than the DELAY and DELEGATE brigade. Margery was definitely the latter so their shift passed smoothly, most of the time.

"I'm rich in years, young at heart and mature of limb," was Margery's introduction the first time they worked together. By then I'd been dumped in a corner, kicked under a table, thrown in a box with comics before coming to rest.

"I'm Francis. It's great to be breathing."

I don't think the women socialised outside the shop but the camaraderie during their shifts was pleasant. Their approaches kept me amused. Francis liked to unpack the mountain of plastic sacks in the back room and speculate on the history of each item. Margery preferred to rummage and imagine what fate had in store for the donation. Francis was quick and practical. Margery dreamed of another life and always asked for Mills and Boon's to be kept to one side. She'd purchase unread titles.

"Imagine life as a princess in an Italian castle, a tall, dark handsome lover…" she'd say to Francis.

"I'm happy enough with a cappuccino and Radio 4."

Margery also made the weakest cup of tea Francis had ever tasted, worse than the hospital's, if that was possible. They shared a hatred of hospitals.

"I've done my time," Margery confided. "Ten years of queuing and probing, it took him that long to rot."

Margery's husband had fought hard but his cancer had declared victory. Margery resolved never to go into another hospital.

"Hospitals out, holidays in," she declared.

Francis agreed. She was planning her first holiday abroad since the all-clear.

"I may not live long," she told her doctor, "but I plan to live well. No more surgery, no further chemo."

She chose not to share her experience. Talking about five years of hell just made you relive it, she reckoned. Why keep going back there? Who really wants to hear about someone else's pain? Emotional self-sufficiency came at a cost but its value was priceless.

Francis was still breathing. She had eyebrows again. Granted she might have only one breast, lost a husband through the process with a sorry-love-can't-deal-with-this declaration and developed a permanent aversion to scarves and bobble hats. DO IT NOW was a good enough motto for the rest of her life.

She poured the tea into her cup and sat down to read me.

"Blissful," she said softly, opening my cover, "to do whatever, whenever."

I guess the life of a newly reconstructed singleton had its perks. Marriage must have its benefits of course but the whiff of boredom that comes from predictability cannot be erased easily, unlike malignant lumps and bumps.

"I plan to cram life," Francis confided to Margery.

"What does that mean?"

"Every evening I sit in my candle-lit bath and reflect on how many first experiences I have achieved that day. Then I smother myself with obscenely expensive unguents that claim to restore my youthful bloom and dream about where next," explained Francis.

I loved to hear about her list, which grew each week from the wild (smoking a spliff from home grown flora), to the whacky (twenty minutes caked in Dead Sea mud warbling along to a frog-croak soundtrack), to the more prosaic (her supermarket's best buy cabernet sauvignon drunk from a crystal brandy balloon).

"All right for some," announced Margery as she breezed into the shop, "ladies who take tea."

"Would you like a cuppa?" asked Francis, standing to switch on the kettle.

"A good find?" Margery asked, gesturing towards me.

"Don't know yet, looks interesting," Francis replied. "It's seen better days, bit damaged."

She held me up so that Margery could see my splattered cover.

"What do you think, paint or wine stains? From an artist's studio?"

I caught the look on Margery's face.

"Where did you find it?"

"Sitting all alone over there on the sorting desk. Nobody loves it."

Francis opened me randomly. Page 218 winked back.

"Story of my great aunt's life!"

"Seriously," said Francis, "this book is a biography of your relative?"

"No," Margery replied, "I don't have a great aunt. I meant not being loved. There's usually a reason why."

"I'm sure for every book, there's a reader just waiting."

"Not that book."

"Margery, even the *Daily Mail* would say that you shouldn't judge a book by its cover."

"The judge did and she got ten years!"

"What are you talking about? A few blotches aren't going to matter. It's in good condition. It's perfectly readable," said Francis. She held me out for inspection. Margery shied away.

"It's not got a fatwa against it."

"You're not wondering why that book ended up in this shop?" asked Margery.

"Hey that's my trick," Francis smiled. "You're the one who usually speculates on who's going to buy it."

"NOBODY is going to touch that book."

Francis stared at Margery and then glanced down at me. She turned to my copyright page.

"It's a first edition," said Francis.

"It's the last. That is definitely not paint."

"Kesia Jaskins has signed the title page."

"Ten years of hospitals and I know what dried blood looks like," said Margery.

Francis sniffed my cover.

"It doesn't smell," she said flicking through the pages before holding it above her head. "Alas, poor book, I read you well!" she misquoted.

"Don't joke about it. It's cursed, Francis. Bin it. Dump it now," Margery whispered.

"Are you crazy?" asked Francis. "It could fetch loads for the charity. A dealer will pay well, even if it's not in pristine condition."

"It was on the news you know," said Margery. "She killed her lover with that book. Hit him on the head."

"The waitress woman?"

Margery nodded her head, "He beat her up. She was pregnant. She went to prison."

"So unfair the way women get treated," said Francis. "It was self-defence. He was always beating her up. Didn't her boss and doctor testify?"

"The lover was a lawyer," said Margery. "The system protects its own. She wasn't the first and she won't be the last. That's what the *Daily Mail* said about it all."

Francis nodded.

Well that's another first, I thought, Francis agreeing with the *Mail*. I wondered how she would reconcile that with her daily sojourn in the bath. Glass of sherry perhaps?

"A truce; it's our last shift together before my holiday in Africa. Let's take a risk. Sit down and I'll read a passage. *Holiday romance*, it's called."

I could only hope my text wasn't going to inspire Francis to have her first holiday love affair.

She opened me at page 218 and began to read aloud:

Holiday romances are all about fantasies. You don't factor in the sunburn and non-delights of sand in your knickers. The sun, sea, sand and pleasures of the flesh are stuffed into memory boxes. The passion doesn't last, the names may be forgotten, the places fade, but the dreams linger of what might have been. Something to remember when it's cold, dark and you're back in the office paying off the credit card.

But there's always that trigger, a glimpse of a colour that takes you back to the beach umbrella, the smell that evokes a face, lustful eyes, a sound that makes you smile and swallow, a Pavlovian response.

It's pineapple for me.

Judas and I flew to The Gambia for a winter break. Our first trip abroad together, courtesy of my editor. In return for a complimentary holiday I agreed to file a feature on the destination. I even found a relevant joke which went something along the lines of a heaven weary God who longed for a quiet, peaceful holiday and asked St Peter for suggestions. All of which were rejected on the grounds of being too extreme – hot, cold, crowded, noisy or isolated. Finally St Peter suggested Earth. Laughing, God responded: "Are you serious? Two thousand years ago I went there, had an affair with some nice Jewish girl, and they're STILL talking about it!"

Judas and I ate pineapple, on the beach, beside the pool, under the stars, in our bed. The fruit was a symbol for hospitality and fertility. We enjoyed its flesh as we licked the dripping juice from each other's bodies. I even returned with my hair flecked with African sunshine and pulled high on my head, pineapple style. Judas dropped a box of chocolate dipped, crystallised pineapple into my Christmas stocking that year. Pina Colada became my cocktail of choice.

I never thought of those hedonistic days as a mere holiday romance. To me they were another building block in our relationship – a sparkle to mark the journey, to differentiate the everyday from the sublime.

Back in London, I attributed the nausea to sunstroke, a hangover and an over indulgence of seafood. It was a shock to hear that pineapple can also be an anthelmintic. When I told Judas I was pregnant, he suggested I use it to induce an abortion.

Would God have said the same to Mary if pineapples had grown in Nazareth?

Something Shared – Pineapple Stuffed with Bacon Risotto

1 large pineapple, washed and split lengthwise
100g Arborio / Carnaroli risotto rice
Small onion, finely chopped
2 sticks celery, finely chopped
12 fine green beans, sliced
3 rashers lean bacon (smoked or unsmoked), diced
10g Parmesan cheese, grated
1 clove garlic, crushed
300ml water with vegetable stock cube
30ml white wine
2 tablespoons olive oil
Salt, pepper to taste
Chopped parsley

1. Discard the pineapple core, scoop out the flesh and pulp.
2. Place the pineapple shells on serving plates, and stabilise by arranging some pulp around bottom of the shells.
3. Add a little olive oil to a large pan.
4. Fry the bacon until lightly brown. Remove from pan.
5. Add the onion and fry until soft, stirring occasionally. Remove from pan.
6. Add the remaining oil and then the rice.
7. Cook for 2 minutes, stir frequently.
8. Add the wine and cook for 1 minute.
9. Then add the vegetable stock stirring frequently.

10. When the liquid has been absorbed by the rice, but it is still moist, add the bacon, celery, green beans, remaining pineapple pulp, garlic, salt and pepper.
11. Add the Parmesan cheese and stir.
12. Remove the pan from the heat and cover. Leave it for three minutes.
13. Warm the pineapple shells in the oven before serving.
14. Spoon the risotto into the pineapple shells and decorate with chopped parsley.

Serves 2

Something Special

Whoa... what a surprise... The Gambia... my second cousin twice removed... sitting there like a Booker prize. Listen you lump of loo paper, I wanted to say. "Show respect." I am a signed first edition of *An Appetite for Words*. You're a mass market pleb, supermarket special print. But hey why go there? KJ, my authorial other half, would cite some adage about the role of elders is to demonstrate an exemplary path to knowledge. Even those magazines she reads over morning coffee advise that you shouldn't judge a book by its cover. Wrinkles or blood splatters, people or paper, experience and class show.

Francis... in case you're wondering how I got from inkjet to jet set... brought me back from the charity shop to her home and stowed me in her backpack. On her do-gooder trip to the dark heat of Africa, she left me, along with a job lot of second hand, children's books in a village school. I've never had much to do with kids. And kids' books don't do it for me – all those pictures, too few words, simple stories about fluffy bunnies and naughty weenies. I'm into language – good grammar, metaphors and similes, punctuation and paragraphs – and proud of it.

So can you imagine what it felt like? Finding another copy of me, in pristine condition, sitting in an African hut with a girl child and her wrinkled minder? Very unsettling, I can tell you.

"Words are sweet but they never take the place of food," read the young one, aloud, in English. "The author says it is an African proverb," she added in her own language.

"Amani, English only," commanded the old woman, sitting cross-legged on the woven mat.

"She maybe not African writer?" asked the girl.

"Perhaps she is not an African writer," corrected the old woman. She shrugged but kept her focus on the half-formed basket nestled between her thighs. Her hands moved swiftly to weave the palm fronds. The girl stroked the page of the book, stained with dark red blotches.

"Bibi, you saying this book be a lie?"

"True for one person. Maybe not true for all people."

Great – here I was, in a strange house, with a kid using me for literacy lessons and a crone who spoke in riddles that only she could answer. What were the odds that two copies of me would end up in this hut? Not that we were the same. The other was pristine, a virgin book. Me, scarred with experience. But Amani had chosen me. Scars showed survival. It had to be a good omen.

"Food ready yet?" the old woman asked. "We eat soon. Books and proverbs can wait."

The English lesson was over.

Amani scampered to find bowls for the porridge made from maize.

"I'm not ready to die from starvation any time soon," Bibi scolded. "Food before sunset."

Amani knelt and took Bibi's hands in her own. She removed the basket from the woman's lap, wiped her hands with cloth, gave her a wooden spoon and guided hand and utensil to the bowl.

"You can taste time," Bibi explained to the child. "Lick under your nose. Taste the dust of the afternoon, sunburnt."

Frankly, I couldn't see that there was much difference. Dust is dust whether it's sprinkled in the morning or settled as evening dirt. I hated the way it settled on my cover. Find your own space, I wanted to say to the irritating stuff. But I guess dust doesn't really impact on blind people in the same way.

"You be quick to smell time," the old woman instructed.

"Fever tree flowers stink stronger at dawn."

"I hate those trees – too many mosquitoes, too much malaria," said Amani.

"Listen, you can hear time," Bibi continued. "Bees here in the morning, monkeys scream at lunch, cicadas shriek in the evening."

Amani would miss her when she went to England. Bibi spoke only when she had something to say. Questions were for young people. Bibi did not always choose to answer.

"Will Aunty be wise like you Bibi?"

"Wisdom is like fire. People take it from others."

"Is Aunty real family?"

"Family is not a month's work."

"How did you meet my Aunty Ruth?"

"A stick is straightened when it is still young."

More riddles and elusive answers. Poor Amani, that sort of advice might make her think her sponsor was going beat her when she arrived in England.

"Where does my Aunty Ruth live? In a house? In a hut? Does she own lots of books? Is she rich? How does she dress? Will she wear silk panties, like the ones she sends to me for my birthday?"

"Too many things belong to people who are greedy," was all Bibi was prepared to reply.

Despite the questions, it seemed that Aunty Ruth was a name not a topic, a direction not a detail, a link not a destination.

Amani had packed her suitcase, a battered gift from the village, discarded by a tourist, rescued and recycled. The letter said she was allowed twenty kilos of luggage.

"So much," said Amani. "All our possessions together wouldn't weigh that much."

There was no need to bring clothes. Aunty Ruth would provide. Shopping, the letter said, they would do together, after arrival. Amani had only been shopping for clothes once in her life. When there were no shoes to fit from the village pile, Bibi took her granddaughter to market – the noise, the smells, hundreds of hawkers, their wares spewed onto pavements in the big town. So many shoes, Amani could scarcely believe her eyes. All colours, all sizes, plain, bows, beads, straps, how would she choose? She didn't. Bibi found them. Boots, lace-ups, thick soles.

"Good for walking. Safe for feet," declared Bibi.

"At least they're yellow."

"A tree is known by its fruit," Bibi said, following the girl's gaze to the red, high-heeled patent pair.

The village had provided a dress for her journey. Another tourist donation but this time it was pretty and looked new. Flowers all over. Not the gaudy, luscious petals of the tropics. Small, pale, feeble flowers in blues and pinks, English not African. The dress had a tie that Bibi fashioned into a bow.

"This dress must have belonged to a movie star," said Amani in wonder.

She picked me and my virgin relation up and said, "Bibi, I have a plan for the books."

The old woman said nothing. She scraped the porridge bowl with her fingers.

"Waste not, want not, is a foreigner proverb. What do they know? You remember Amani, waste never, want forever."

"We have two copies of this book. One for me, one for you."

"Nothing occurs that has not occurred," Bibi replied. "I do not need a book."

"I want to leave you a copy of this book. Then we will be connected, you and me, here and there. Power shared."

"The lion's power lies in our fear of him."

210

"Here is the book," Amani said, placing my second cousin, twice removed, into Bibi's hands. The old woman explored its shape, size and texture, thumb and first finger savouring the touch.

"It smells new," she said.

"It is signed by the author, Kesia Jaskins. Lots of wise words, African proverbs and all."

"As long as you live you will learn."

I knew that the Ruth of whom Amani dreamed would make sure the future smiled kindly. A good school, a private tutor, perhaps even a university education.

"Maybe Aunty will know Kesia Jenkins?"

"Let me have the other copy," demanded Bibi. The girl gave me to her. The gnarled hands felt my pages, smelt my cover, over and over again.

Amani did not ask questions.

"Patience can cook a stone."

The old woman clutched me close to her body and placed my stained cover against her heart.

"This book is for me. Much blood, many tears. You take the new copy, new life, new beginnings, new people."

"Bibi, tell me the story of your book," Amani begged.

The old woman beckoned and the girl moved to lie on the mat beside her.

"Proverbs are the daughters of experience," Bibi began as she stroked my pages. "This book has had two parents, one who stayed with the words, the other ran away. This book has many mothers, not all gave birth to words, wisdom or babies.

In the beginning was the birth mother. Her name be Kesia. Your Aunty Ruth will know the story. She will tell you it sometime, maybe while I breathe, maybe not. England will show you many books, many true things, not all good, not all happy.

The birth father is distant, a memory in the book. Dead or alive, he no matter. He be a raindrop on the journey, starting the seed, nothing more."

My pages quivered under the weight of that old lady's prophecy. I had to acknowledge that wisdom isn't always recorded in books.

"You remember your name means peace?" asked Bibi.

Amani nodded.

"Your copy of the book will bring peace. Kesia needs Amani. Many other mothers have read this copy that I keep. Mothers with their own ideas of peace. One through death. Her story be these blood scars. You have no need to meet these other mothers. You will be their peace. They not yours. Read the book. Think about the words. Be they wise for you? Be they true for the Kesia writer lady who is not African but knows this land? You take the clean book, the fresh paper, the no stink of life, no lived-in copy. I will keep the pain of this other book with me. It will find its peace with me."

When Bibi placed me beside her, I had a bad feeling. Did she plan to burn me as soon as the child flew off? I had heard her say many times that bad things needed to be destroyed in order to protect the future.

"Innocence is precious," I heard her mutter.

Amani picked up her pristine book.

"Aunty Ruth and the famous writer, be they family to each other?" asked Amani.

"One be white with an African heart. One be African but lives white."

"Bibi, not another riddle!"

And though I could guess the plot a book can only await its fate. The writer and the reader determine who, what, when and where next. My bet was that Ruth, her soon-to-be-met sponsor, would ensure Kesia Jaskins crossed paths with Amani.

So you wouldn't read about as they say. A kid, a granny and I know the mum – you couldn't make it up. Certainly a publisher would reject such a story as too contrived. But didn't someone say truth is stranger than fiction?

Just as she was about to pack the book in her suitcase, Bibi did the unthinkable.

"What words be written on the last page of that book?"

A question, in English. The getting of wisdom was not going to be so one-sided from now. I wondered what the chances were for a happy ending.

Amani, startled by the request, smiled at her grandmother and began to read:

> *"We are all born originals – why is it so many of us die copies?"*
>
> *Not my words but those of an old English poet, Edward Young, born in 1681. It is unusual but not original to get pregnant by a priest. Following in a long line of women who have been surprised to end up as single mothers when they were expecting marriage, mortgage and motherhood, I copied their strategies and survived. The lesson was universal, the original rule.*
>
> *My baby taught me what I most needed to learn. Her physical presence in my life may have been short. Her lesson was eternal and simple. Real love is unconditional. Until I became a mother I had no idea such love existed. I may have left the convent a mother without a baby but the secret shared by the motherhood mafia is imbedded. The unconditional love genome – fathomless, unquantifiable, overwhelmingly intense, sciatica-sharp, painful, pleasurable, complete, forever flowing outwards from your core.*

Judas' sister became the original guardian angel. When I wept, she folded me in her arms, my tears soaking her shoulders. When I was depressed, she fed me hope; anger was stroked with kindness; vengeance coaxed into acceptance. If there had been any justice in the world that year, Judas would have been struck by lightning, his sister would have been nominated for Pope and I would have morphed into a peek-a-boo on demand.

My culture suggests that justice is about balancing the injustice of the perpetrator against the hurt and need of the victim. But who was the real victim in this contested territory? Me with my love-conquers-all naivety? Judas with his sacred-sex conflict of interest? My daughter who needed stability and mature love to nurture her development? Mother, father or baby – whose needs, whose hurts – what balance? True justice, it seemed to me, was really about obligation. The baby first, the baby second, the baby forever commanded my judgmental conscience.

In the years that followed I tried to copy the example set by Judas' sister. She worked with women in need. I learnt that meeting another's need solves your own. I support fifteen abandoned girls in orphanages throughout Africa. Their dreams may become their tomorrows.

My greatest hope is, that before I die, I meet the original. My daughter – a surprise, the blend of us both, something special.

Something Special – Frozen surprise

50g meringue, crumbled
500ml double cream
250ml single cream
2 tablespoons of Marsala or sweet liqueur
Handful of unsalted pistachio nuts
3 passion fruit

1. Combine all the ingredients except the passion fruit in a freezer proof container. Stir well.
2. Cut the passion fruit in half and scoop out the flesh and seeds.
3. Keep half of the fruit pulp and set aside.
4. Add the remaining half of the fruit pulp to the mixture and stir through to create swirls.
5. Place the mixture in the freezer overnight.
6. To serve, leave out of the freezer for 15 minutes, scoop into glasses and decorate with the retained fruit pulp.

Serves 4

ABOUT THE AUTHOR

Dianne Stadhams is an Australian, resident in the UK, who works globally in marketing and project management. With a PhD in visual anthropology she has spent many years using creative tools – drama, dance, radio, video – to empower others in some of the world's poorest nations. She believes passionately that the arts are valuable tools to promote social cohesion, provoke debate and influence attitudes and mind sets.

She has had a number of short stories published in the following anthologies: *Crackers* (2018), *Glit-e-rary* (2017), *Baubles* (2016), *Snowflakes* (2015), *Recognition* (2009); two novels shortlisted for the Triskele Global Competitions: *Doll Face* (2018) and *Crocodile Tears* (2016); two plays selected by Bristol Old Vic for workshop development: *Never Black or White* (2017) and *Aftermath* (2016); *Sh*t* was selected for a workshop production at the Croydon Warehouse in 2004.

Screen scripts include *Tada the Dancing Drum* (television series to promote literacy in Africa 2010): *Pascale's People* (Dulwich Festival London, Creteil International Festival of Women in Film, France 2005): *Tourism in The Gambia*, a television documentary made with and for Gambia Television (screened at Royal Anthropological Institute's International Film Festival, Le Festival du Quartier Film Festival Senegal 2003 and Italian Ethnographic International Film Festival 2004): *Beyond the Brochure* (Toura D'Ora International Film Festival, Germany 2001).

www.stadhams.com